AND I UNSTOPPABLE

Also by Amanda Flower

Andi Boggs Series

Andi Unexpected

Andi Under Pressure

Appleseed Creek Mystery Series

A Plain Death

A Plain Scandal

A Plain Disappearance

A Plain Malice

India Hayes Mystery Series

Maid of Murder

Murder in a Basket

Living History Mystery Series

The Final Reveille

Amish Quilt Shop Mystery Series

(writing as Isabella Alan)

Plainly Murder

Murder, Plain and Simple

Murder, Simply Stitched

Murder, Served Simply

Murder, Plainly Read

AN ANDI BOGGS NOVEL

AMANDA FLOWER

ZONDERKIDZ

Andi Unstoppable
Copyright © 2015 by Amanda Flower

This title is also available as a Zondervan eBook.
Visit www.zondervan.com/ebooks

Requests for information should be addressed to:
Zonderkidz, 3900 Sparks Dr. SE, Grand Rapids, Michigan 49546

ISBN 978-0-310-73766-7

Cover illustration: Chris Coady
Cover design: Deborah Washburn
Interior design: David Conn

Printed in the United States of America

15 16 17 18 19 20 21 /DCI/ 20 19 18 17 16 15 14 13 12 11 10 9 8 7 6 5 4 3 2 1

For my birders
Andrew Flower
and
Sarah Preston

CASE FILE NO. 1

When a teacher claps his hands at the beginning of class, I consider it a warning for a big announcement. Until our Life Science teacher, Mr. McCone opened his mouth, I didn't know if the announcement was going to be good or bad. The final bell that told us it was the beginning of the last period of the day rang, and Mr. McCone clapped his hands for a second time. "Simmer down! Simmer down! I have news."

Suddenly, the room was so quiet I could hear the boy in the seat behind me breathing. I scooted forward in my desk.

The science teacher was a short, round man who had puffy dark hair that reminded me of feathers. He beamed happily. Actually, Mr. McCone was always beaming. In the three short weeks I'd been a student at Killdeer Middle School, I hadn't seen a frown on his face or heard him raise his voice. That included the handful of times he'd asked a student to go out in the hall, which didn't happen often because who would want to misbehave in Mr. McCone's class?

"I have super news," the science teacher said. "Fall migration is here!"

Silence fell on the classroom as we tried to figure out what this meant. Migration? Migration of what?

"Does anyone know what that means?" the science teacher asked.

My best friend Colin Carter's hand shot up so fast his floppy brown bangs fluttered on his forehead. Of course, Colin would know. Colin knew everything. He was a good guy to have around during a trivia game.

Mr. McCone called on him. "Colin?"

Colin lowered his hand. "It's the birds. Songbirds and waterfowl fly to their winter homes. Many travel hundreds or even thousands of miles to reach their final destinations."

"Exactly. This year the migration is even more exciting, and today I learned the most wonderful news." Mr. McCone lowered his voice. "A Kirtland's warbler was spotted in the Shalley Park woods."

A hush fell over the classroom. I don't know about the other kids, but I was quiet because I was trying to decide what that exactly meant and why it was so exciting. Colin didn't even raise his hand.

Finally, Ava Gomez, sitting in the center seat, front row, spoke up without raising her hand. Ava never raised her hand. She thought she was above being called on. "What's so special about a Kirtland's warbler?"

The seventh grade science teacher put a hand to his chest, like she'd struck him with a bullet and not a question. "It's rare, very rare, indeed, especially in Ohio. There hasn't been one spotted around in Carroll County in over twenty years. Many birders would give their life savings just for a glimpse of a Kirtland's, which is why at this very moment dozens of birders are on their way to Killdeer. The news of the sighting has spread like wildfire across the birder community. Bird fever is here in little Killdeer, Ohio."

"They are coming here to Killdeer?" a boy in the back of the classroom asked. "No one comes to Killdeer. I mean other than the college students going to Michael Pike University, and they hardly ever leave campus."

"Yes, they are." Mr. McCone rubbed his hands together a second time and his eyes sparkled with excitement. He was really working the mad scientist angle. "Now, I have had a brilliant idea. We'll skip ahead in our current lesson plans and jump to ornithology for the next two weeks because I have the best assignment planned. You will love it!"

Someone behind me, probably the same boy who questioned anyone coming to Killdeer, mumbled, "The guy's a nut."

Ava flipped her long straight black hair, hair I envied as it was a daily struggle to get my curly, strawberry blonde—AKA pink—hair into a ponytail. "But

Mr. McCone, we are still studying mollusks. What about the rest of the invertebrates? How can we skip invertebrates and go right to birds? The class will have no basis to study the bird's anatomy. Of course, I will because I have done extensive study of all animal kingdoms on my own time."

"Suck up," the boy behind me said.

Mr. McCone laughed. "Oh, the snails will be there when we are ready to come back to them. They aren't very fast."

The class groaned.

"On the other hand," Mr. McCone said, "fall migration only passes through our area for a couple of weeks. We can't miss the opportunity to study birds, especially those as rare as the Kirtland's warbler, in the field." He clasped his hands together behind his back and started to pace. "Now for the assignment. You will be put into teams of two, and in your teams you'll observe as many birds as you can for the next two weeks, starting tomorrow. The assignment will be worth eighty points. The team that sees the most birds will receive an additional ten points." He paused. "And the team that brings me a photograph of the Kirtland's warbler in the wild will earn an additional twenty points! Doesn't that sound awesome?"

Some adults just couldn't pull off the use of the word "awesome" convincingly. Mr. McCone was one of them.

Craig, who was also in my gym class, raised his hand from the second row. "What about the ghost?"

I laughed, but I realized that no one else in the

classroom was joining me. "There's a ghost?" I asked without raising my hand. If Ava could do it, so could I.

Mr. McCone leaned on his desk. "It's local folklore. Every small town needs its tall tale."

"It's not just a story. I heard all about it," a girl kitty-corner to me said. "It's a lady ghost, and she wanders the park in the early morning and evening, looking for her lost loved ones. My dad told me he saw her while he was cutting through the park when he was a kid. She was as white as a sheet, and she was moaning."

A shiver ran down my spine. Ghosts weren't real. I had no reason to be afraid of a story.

Ava whipped around in her seat. "That is the dumbest thing I have ever heard, Courtney. Aren't you too old to believe ghost stories?"

"It's true," Courtney said. "My dad told me."

"Your dad lied," Ava shot back.

Courtney glared at her. "My dad doesn't lie."

"Then he thought he saw something. Sometimes that happens when people aren't thinking logically."

Courtney jumped out of her seat. "Are you saying he's crazy?"

Ava shrugged.

Courtney, who was twice the size of Ava, looked as if she was ready to charge the smaller girl.

Mr. McCone stood up and stepped between them. "Girls, girls, there's no reason to argue."

Courtney slid back behind her desk.

"Yes, I know there have been rumors about the ghost, but if she comes out in the early morning and at night, simply don't go into the woods then if you're afraid." The teacher smiled as if he had solved the problem.

Ava looked as if she wanted to say something more, but the science teacher said, "First things first, I need to break you into pairs. You will meet with your partner and together plan how you'll reach your birding goal." His eyes glowed and reminded me of my aunt Amelie's cat. Mr. Rochester's eyes gleamed at night when he stared out the window at some unseen mouse or mole.

Another hand shot into the air. "But Mr. McCone, there are twenty-one kids in the class. What will happen to the extra person?"

Mr. McCone nodded. "Yes, yes, that is a problem. Break up into pairs, and we will see who is leftover."

The sound of scraping filled the classroom as kids leapt out of their seats. No one wanted to be the one "leftover." I knew I had nothing to worry about. Colin was the smartest kid in seventh grade and my best friend. He would be my partner. Colin was always my partner.

I waited until my classmates were done jumping over each other before I quietly stood up and walked to Colin's desk on the other side of the classroom. He wasn't alone.

Petite, raven-haired Ava Gomez glared down at Colin, who was sitting at his desk, with her hands on her hips. "What do you mean *I don't know*?"

"What's going on?" I asked.

"I . . ." Colin gave me a panicked look.

"Colin is going to be my birding partner," Ava said.

She arched an eyebrow at me. I hated that she could do that—I'd spent hours trying in the mirror, but all I ended up doing was looking totally confused.

Colin's eyes widened, but he didn't correct her. He was far too nice to tell anyone, even my arch-nemesis, he wouldn't be her partner. That was left up to me.

I folded my arms. "Colin is working with me."

"Really?" Ava smiled. "Did you ask him to be your partner? Because I didn't see you ask him. How self-centered of you to assume you and Colin would be partners. If I were Colin I wouldn't want to be taken for granted so much."

I pushed my frizzy hair behind my ear. "Well, it's a good thing that you're not Colin, and I don't take him for granted."

"Oh really?" Ava asked. "Colin, do you think Andi takes your friendship for granted?"

Colin's hair fell into his glasses as his neck whipped back and forth between Ava and me. "I ... I ..."

Mr. McCone clapped his hands, which made Ava and me jump. We hadn't even known that he was there. "This solves our problem. Ava and Andi, you will both be Colin's partner for the project. This will avoid the embarrassment of an odd man out. I was always the last one picked for kickball in school, and I know how hard it can be to be the low man on the totem pole."

It was no surprise to anyone that Mr. McCone was chosen last in kickball. He looked like he would be the last pick for everything with the exception of maybe a spelling bee.

"What?!" the three of us cried at the same time.

The teacher adjusted his glasses. "Would one of you rather work alone?"

There was silence. None of us was going to volunteer to work by ourselves. More people meant we had more chances to see birds and maybe even see the Kirtland's warbler that was worth an additional twenty points.

"No," Ava and I mumbled.

"Good. I'm going to expect great things from this group made up of three of my star pupils." He sauntered away to the next pair of students.

Ava and I glared at each other for a full minute after Mr. McCone moved on.

Colin sighed. "If we're going to get an 'A' on this project, we'll have to work together."

I sighed. Colin was right. I wasn't going to let Ava Gomez stand between me and a good grade. "When should we start?"

"Tonight," Colin said. "We can meet at my house after school to make a plan. It's Thursday, so we should spend Saturday at the park looking for birds. If the Kirtland's is still there, we have to see it."

Life Science was the last class of the day, which meant we could get to work right away. I nodded. "Sounds good to me."

Ava frowned. "I can't go right after school. I'll meet you at your house later."

"Why?" I asked.

Her jaw twitched. "There's something I have to do first, and I don't know if I can look for birds on Saturday yet either. It depends."

"Depends on what?" I asked.

"Some of us have other responsibilities that are none of your business." She glared at me. "I'll meet you at Colin's house later and let you know about Saturday then."

I folded my arms. "If you have to ask your mom for permission, we get that. It's not like we're going to run off into the woods without telling our families."

"I don't have to ask my mom," Ava said through gritted teeth.

Colin opened his mouth as if he were about to ask another question, but snapped it shut as soon as he saw Ava's glare.

The bell rang, and Ava grabbed her backpack from the floor. "I have to go." She fled the room. Colin and I were much slower in gathering our things.

"I wonder what that was about," Colin said.

I hoisted my backpack onto my shoulders. "Let's see if she shows up tonight like she promised."

Mr. McCone was right. Bird fever had over-taken Killdeer. As Colin and I rode our bikes home after school, we saw dozens of men and women, mostly older adults, wandering downtown holding binoculars to their eyes. Local shopkeepers stood outside too, staring at the binocular-people like Martians had invaded and they were still trying to decide if they came in peace.

I rode up next to Colin. He slowed his pedaling to match mine. "Where are they all going to sleep?" I asked.

Colin adjusted the rearview mirror attached to his bike helmet. "That's a good question. I hope Bergita doesn't offer our house. My parents would freak."

I let my bike cruise behind Colin again, and we coasted down Dunlap Avenue to our houses. Mine was a large Dutch colonial that had been in the family for five generations. My aunt Amelie inherited it from her parents and moved in when she got a job as an English professor at Michael Pike University just a few blocks away. Two years later, my older sister Bethany and I moved in after the death of both of our parents. Mom and Dad were botanists and had been in Central America looking for plants when their small plane crashed into the mountains on the border of Guatemala and Belize. That was almost nine months ago now. Sometimes it felt like it had been years since they died, and sometimes it felt like it was that morning.

An old VW bus was in Colin's driveway. It was rusty and powder blue and a huge dent marred the rear fender.

"Whose car is that?" I asked Colin.

Colin grinned. "You'll see." He sped away from me.

I pedaled faster to catch up. "Can you tell me if it's good news or bad news that that car—or whatever it is—is in your driveway?"

Colin glanced over his shoulder as he swung his bike into the Carters' driveway. "Depends on who you ask. My dad would say it was trouble."

Before I could ask Colin what he meant by that, his front screen door banged against the house. Colin's pug Jackson shot out the door as if someone had zapped him with a hundred volts of electricity in his curled tail.

A woman filled the doorway. Her hands were on her hips and her shoulders were as wide as the door. She wore tan shorts and a blue sweatshirt. The sweatshirt asked, "Got birds?" Her gray hair was shaved close to her head, and she wore a camo-pattern scarf tied into a knot around her thick neck.

Jackson dove under the nearest bush.

"Colin Thomas Carter," the woman bellowed. "Get up here and give this old woman a hug."

A dog up the street howled at her shouts.

Colin dropped his bike and, with the hugest grin on his face I had ever seen, ran up the three steps to the porch. The giant woman wrapped her arms around him and squeezed so tight I had to look away just in case she crushed Colin's bones. Finally, she let him go. "Are you still getting straight A's?" she asked.

Colin nodded but didn't answer, probably because she squeezed all the wind out of him. I was impressed he was still upright after that hug.

"Good." She let go of his shoulders. "If I ever hear about your grades slipping, you will have to answer to me, understood?"

Colin nodded dumbly again.

She examined me over his head. "You must be Andi. I have heard quite a bit about you from my sister and my nephew here. Quite a bit. You've led Colin into some tight scrapes these last few months."

I opened my mouth to argue. The scrapes Colin and I had had been a team effort. I didn't make him do anything he didn't want to, and we hadn't done anything too dangerous ... at least not that often.

The woman let go of Colin. "Come up here so I can give you a hug too."

I hesitated. A cracked rib didn't sound like that much fun to me.

"I won't bite," she said.

I dropped my backpack next to my bike and climbed up the steps. The woman wrapped me into a surprisingly gentle hug. I hugged her back even though I still had no idea who she was.

"Andi," Colin said after the large women let me go. "This is my great-aunt Claudette. She's my grandma Bergita's sister."

Claudette punched her fists into her wide hips. "Did you have to add the great on there? I refuse to be old and the great makes me sound old."

Colin laughed. "You're not old, Claudette."

She pointed a finger at him. "You got that right, and I have no intention of ever being old."

"What are you doing here?" Colin asked. "You haven't come to visit in ages."

She nodded. "I know. I should visit more often, but the birds are always calling me. Who knew that they would call me here?"

"You're birding?" Colin asked. "In Killdeer?"

She nodded as she placed a hand on his shoulder. "Yep, and I'll be here for a few days. Bergita will break the news to your parents."

"You came because of the Kirtland's warbler?" I asked.

Claudette's entire face lit up when I mentioned the Kirtland's. It reminded me of Colin's when he had a new and exciting idea to share. Even though she was his great aunt, it was easy to see the two of them were related. "Yes. That's exactly why I'm here. I shouldn't be a bit surprised that the two of you know about it too considering how smart Bergita claims you are."

Colin's grandmother Bergita came out the front door. "Oh good. You're home from school. Andi, I see you have had a chance to meet my sister. I hope she didn't squeeze you too tight. Her hugs are known to be dangerous."

Claudette snorted. "Don't scare the poor girl."

Bergita laughed. "Andi, why don't you run over to your house and ask Bethany if she wants to come over for a bit too? Amelie called me and she's going to be home late from work, so I'm inviting you girls over for dinner."

I tried to hide my frown. Amelie always called and said that she was going to be late. There always seemed to be a meeting or a paper to grade that kept her on campus just a bit longer. "Bethany isn't going to want to come over." I knew my sister. She was probably already online Skyping with one of her friends from our old school. Bethany hated Killdeer and was already counting the days until she graduated high school and could leave, and she was only in the ninth grade.

Bergita folded her arms. "Ask her anyway. Bethany shouldn't spend so much time alone in the house."

I sighed. "Okay." I would much rather have stayed at the Carters' and learned about Colin's birding great-aunt Claudette. If she helped us look for the Kirtland's, we would definitely earn all the extra credit points.

On the way across the yard to my driveway, I picked up my bike and backpack. I parked the bike in the garage and headed inside. Mr. Rochester greeted me at the front door with a yowl. Unlike my sister, he hated to be shut up alone in the house all day. I scratched him under the chin. "Want an afternoon snack, Mr. Rochester?"

He began to purr. I took that as a 'yes.' I dropped my backpack on the couch and headed to the kitchen where Bethany sat on the counter eating Doritos. Her long legs hung over the counter and the heels of her feet beat a rhythm into the cupboard below. She licked Dorito cheese from her fingers. "What are you all excited about?"

"Who said I was excited?" I asked as I removed the cat treats from the overhead cupboard. We had to keep them there because somehow Mr. Rochester had figured out how to open the lower cupboards with his paws. We discovered this after he had gotten sick from eating an entire box of cat treats that Amelie had hidden under the sink.

Bethany rolled her eyes. "I can tell when you're hyper about something. What happened at school? Did you win the science fair or something?"

It wasn't often my older sister asked me what I was up to, so I didn't want to jinx it. "Have you seen the birders in town?"

"Huh?"

"The birders," I said. "Didn't you see people with binoculars wandering around downtown when you walked home from school?"

"Well, yeah," she admitted. "But I thought it was a bunch of lost old people. Maybe they escaped from a nursing home."

I sighed. "No, those are birders. They're here because a really rare bird, a Kirtland's warbler, was seen in the Shalley Park woods. People are coming from all over to catch a glimpse of it. Colin and I are going to find it. If we get a photograph of it, we'll earn twenty extra credit points on our science project."

"You're all jazzed up because you can get extra credit for a class you are already acing? That's overkill in my opinion."

I dropped the treats on the floor for Mr. Rochester. The orange tabby pounced on them. "Then, I guess it's good I didn't ask your opinion."

Bethany snorted.

"Amelie is going to be late, so Bergita sent me over here to ask if you want to go over there for dinner."

"What else is new? Tell Bergita I'm fine with my Doritos."

"Bergita's sister, Claudette, is there right now. She's a big-time birder and came to town to see the Kirtland's."

"I'll pass. I'm not that interested in listening to you all talk about birds."

I grabbed a package of fruit snacks from the cupboard for myself and shrugged as if I didn't care. "Fine. I'm going to Colin's."

"Are you and Colin going to have one of your little investigations about the birds?" She smirked. "You're in seventh grade now, Andi. Don't you think you're a little old to be playing detective?"

I gritted my teeth. "This isn't an investigation."

At the time, I had been telling the truth.

I stomped from the kitchen and headed to my attic bedroom. Mr. Rochester always knew when I was headed upstairs. He beat me every time no matter where he was in the house.

I climbed the second set of stairs to my room. When my dad was growing up in the old Boggs family home, the attic had been his room. With Colin's help, I had spent most of the summer turning the neglected space back into a bedroom.

I threw my backpack on my bed and took out my books. I would need to pack for the birding expedition.

The only item that I knew I definitely would need was binoculars. I knelt down and yanked out a plastic box from under the bed. I sat back on my heels. Mr. Rochester leaned over the bed and watched me. I eyed him. "I don't know if I'm ready to see this stuff," I confided to the orange tabby.

The box contained some of my parents' things that I saved from our old house. Bethany insisted that she didn't want anything from our parents, but I had kept a few memories that weren't worth anything to anyone but me. I knew Amelie saved some items for Bethany too. She was waiting to give them to my sister at "the right time."

"Here goes," I said after a deep breath.

I opened the box and the smell of my father's soap hit me like a bowling ball directly to the stomach. I tried not to look at any of the items in the box for long and just find what I needed. I rooted through the box until I came up with Dad's binoculars. As soon as I found them, I ripped them from the box, slammed the box shut, and shoved it back underneath the bed. I did it all so fast that Mr. Rochester meowed in protest.

I fell backward onto my butt and caught my breath. Mr. Rochester jumped on the floor and nosed my arm, purring softly. I don't know if he did that to comfort me or himself. I wiped a tear from my eye that I hadn't even known was there. The binoculars were in my lap. They were high-powered but lighter than you would think. My father had used them on his research trips dozens of times, and they were the only item that came back from their last trip to Central America.

I shoved the binoculars into my backpack and was about to head for the stairs when I decided to take one more thing. The casebook. Colin and I hadn't used it since the summer, when we solved a case on Michael

Pike's campus. I told Bethany that Colin and I weren't on a case, but it couldn't hurt to take the casebook with me.

I gave Mr. Rochester one more pat on the head before I left my bedroom. Outside, I ran across the front lawn from my yard to Colin's. Colin was waiting for me on the front porch, standing in front of the door.

I skipped up the three steps.

Colin didn't open the door.

I held onto the straps of my pack. "What's going on? Why don't we go in?"

"We will. I have to warn you. Claudette can be a little intense." He wrinkled his nose.

I laughed and adjusted my backpack higher up on my shoulder. "I got that when I met her. I saw her almost squeeze you to death, remember?"

"Yeah," he said. "But she can be really intense about birds. I mean, this is her life, so just watch what you say about them to her."

I rolled my eyes. "It's not like I'm going to start insulting cardinals or something. Can we go in now?"

He nodded and opened the door. I followed him through the living room into the kitchen. The Carters' kitchen was the biggest room in their house, which was good because it was where Bergita spent most of her time baking.

In the kitchen, Bergita and her sister sat at the table. The most surprising thing about the two sisters was how little they looked alike. Claudette was wide and had that buzzed hair while Bergita was tall and lanky. She divided her white hair into pigtails and wore denim overalls over a tie-dye T-shirt.

A large map was spread in front of them on the table. Claudette stabbed her blunt index finger onto the table with so much force I was surprised she didn't break it. Her features were squished together and red, reminding me of the inside of a tomato. "Bergita, I can take care of myself. I always have."

Bergita sighed. "I know you have, but you aren't getting any younger. Shouldn't you be thinking about your future? You have spent every penny you have searching the globe for birds. I'm afraid you will have nothing left to live off of. I had to send you money to fly home from Papua, New Guinea last month, didn't I?"

"You won't have to do that again. I'll find the money."

"I don't mind helping," Bergita said. "But—"

Claudette glared at her older sister. "You don't know what birding means to me. You never have. It's *everything* to me."

"I know—"

"I don't want to talk about it any longer." She jabbed her finger into the large map stretched across the table again. "This is where we should start our search. *This* is where we'll find the Kirtland's."

"Did you ask if we could go with them?" I whispered to Colin.

That was a mistake.

Claudette's head snapped in our direction so fast that her glasses flew off her face and fell to the tabletop. Without missing a beat, she snatched them off the map and put them back on her nose. "I'm glad to see you are back, but no one said you're going with me to see the Kirtland's. This is serious business, not child's play. I can't have anyone slowing me down."

I glanced at Colin. "Did you tell them about the assignment?"

Colin flushed. "I didn't get a chance."

Bergita smiled. "What assignment? Something for school?"

I nodded and told them about the birding homework we had.

Claudette smacked the table, and the rest of us jumped. "Hot dog! I'm glad the public school system is finally paying attention to something important like birds."

I climbed on a barstool beside the counter. "If we went birding with you, we would be sure to see the Kirtland's and a whole bunch of other birds."

Claudette frowned just for a moment, and I thought she was going to say 'no.' Instead she said, "I'm not one to discourage budding birders. Two capable kids like you shouldn't be too much extra trouble. Yes, you can come with me, but you have to do everything I say to do in the field. Do you understand?"

Colin and I nodded.

Bergita left the table and walked to the counter where she started to dice a tomato. A large salad bowl sat next to her cutting board with lettuce, peppers, and mushrooms already cut into it. "This is going to be a great adventure for us all," Bergita said as if she hadn't just been in an argument with her sister. "I've accompanied my sister on her birding trips a couple of times but never in my hometown." She glanced up from her tomatoes. "Where's Bethany?"

"She's happy with her Doritos," I said.

Bergita shook her head and continued to dice.

"If you're going to go out into the field with us, you need to know the plan. We'll go into the park this way and camp near the old Shalley homestead." Claudette ran her finger along a trail in the map. I could see that the trail split Shalley Park in two.

"Shalley homestead?" I spun around in my stool to see Claudette better. "Is that where the ghost lives?"

Claudette's head jerked up. "Don't tell me you listen to those ridiculous stories. I will not tolerate any silly ghost talk on my birding trip."

Bergita chuckled. "That ghost story has been around a long time. I remember hearing it as a little girl."

"What's the story?" I asked.

The doorbell rang and interrupted us. "That must be Ava," Colin said.

Bergita put down her knife. "You invited Ava here?"

"She's in our birder group too." I jumped off the stool and followed Colin.

Claudette called behind me. "I hope you kids can keep up."

Colin threw open the door. Jackson, who was snoozing on the couch, barely lifted his head.

Through the front door, I saw Ava's brother's red pickup truck idling on the street. "Does your brother want to come in too?"

Ava frowned at me. "No. Romero has other stuff he needs to do. He'll be back in an hour to pick me up."

When Ava stepped into Colin's home, she looked at everything as though she was taking inventory. She pursed her lips together as if she didn't like what she saw. I didn't know what was wrong with it. It was an ordinary living room. Maybe the Drs. Carter had a little too much beige in the place, but it was perfectly tidy.

"An hour doesn't give us much time to plan," Colin said.

She folded her arms over her notebook. "That's all the time I have. I have other stuff to do tonight."

"What stuff?" I asked. "What could be more important than this birding project right now?"

Ava scowled at me. "We're wasting time. I now have fifty-eight minutes. My brother will be back right at five thirty."

"Okay, okay," I said. "Let's go to the kitchen and introduce you to Claudette. Great news! Colin's great-aunt—don't let her hear you say 'great' about her—is an expert birder, and she is going to take us out in the field to find the Kirtland's."

Colin waved us across the room. "We've already told Bergita and Claudette about our assignment, and they're on board."

When we walked into the kitchen, Bergita pointed to the pizza on the counter. "Ava, I'm so glad you could come over."

Ava squinted at Colin's grandmother as if she was trying to decide if the older woman was lying to her.

Bergita simply smiled. "I just pulled this out of the oven. You kids help yourselves."

I grabbed a piece of pepperoni pizza and placed it on a plate before slipping back onto the stool at the counter. I spun the seat so that I faced Claudette and the map.

Colin and Ava did the same and perched on stools on either side of me.

Claudette sat at the dining table and seemed to have no interest in the pizza. She made notes on a yellow legal pad. "Since there will be a group of us going out, we have to rethink our supply list. We should have enough food—I hope you kids like granola—and then there's always the issue of the amount of toilet paper to bring. You never know."

Ava grimaced at her slice of pizza.

"I have an extra tent," Bergita said. "It holds two adults. It should be plenty big enough for the girls. Colin has a single pup tent, so we are good as far as shelter goes."

Great, I'd be sharing a tent with Ava.

Ava wiped her mouth with a napkin. "Why do we need a tent?"

Claudette dropped her legal pad onto the table. "Because we have to be there as early as possible to see the birds. It's best to camp the night before."

"I—I can't do that," Ava stammered.

"Are you afraid of the ghost?" Colin teased.

"No," Ava snapped with her old confidence.

"Yeesh." He held up his hands in surrender. "I was just kidding."

"Well don't," she snapped again.

Claudette pointed her pen at them. "I don't like the sound of this. There will be no squabbles out in the field. Do you hear me?"

We all nodded. Ava was tough, but Claudette—she was tougher.

Ava wrinkled her forehead. "I will have to check and see if I can come. I have some stuff I have to do at night. I'll have to ask my mom."

"Ava, if you need me to talk to your mother about the camping trip, I can," Bergita said.

"No," Ava said, more quietly. "I'll talk to her."

"Okay." Bergita resumed dicing. "What about binoculars? Does everyone have those?"

Colin and I nodded, but Ava shook her head.

Bergita smiled. "That works out well because I just so happen to have an extra pair." She dumped the last of the tomatoes into the salad bowl and walked across the room to the buffet, which ran along the wall. Usually, the buffet was covered with Bergita's best dishes, the ones no one is allowed to eat on. Now, in the dishes' place there was everything a camper would need for a night in the wild.

I popped my last bite of pizza into my mouth and hopped off the stool for a closer look. Ava and Colin did the same, but Colin grabbed another piece of pizza and brought it with him.

Bergita handed Ava a pair of binoculars from the buffet.

"Thank you," Ava mumbled. She said the words like they had actually caused her physical pain.

"Bergita, is that a grappling hook?" Colin asked, pointing at the pointed object in the middle of the buffet.

She winked. "We must always be prepared. We don't know what we are going to come across out there."

Ava looked through her binoculars. "It's Shalley Park, not the Grand Canyon."

Bergita shrugged. "You never know where adventure will lead."

Ava dropped her binoculars from her eyes. "What does the warbler look like?"

"I have it." Claudette flipped through her well-thumbed bird guide and pointed to a page, then handed the book to me.

There were several similar-looking birds on the page. All of them had the same shaped body and at least a little yellow on them. The bird that Claudette pointed out didn't appear that much different from the others. It had a bright yellow underbelly and a bluish-gray back with black markings on the sides of its body. "That's it?" I asked.

Claudette sneered. "What do you mean 'that's it?'"

I licked my lips. "I thought it would be more impressive. Rainbow colored or a crest of feathers shooting out from the top of its head? Maybe something a little more interesting?"

Claudette took the bird book from my hand. "First of all, it's a real bird, not a Dr. Seuss character, and it sounds to me like you are thinking of a painted bunting. You won't see any of those around here. They live in the southern part of the country. Second of all, didn't you notice the bright colors on this bird? It's beautiful. I have waited my entire life to see it. Finally, I have my best chance." There was awe in her voice.

"You've never seen one before?" Colin asked.

The lines around Claudette's mouth deepened. "No."

"Oh," I said.

Claudette slammed the book closed. "While the three of you are in school tomorrow, I will do some preliminary birding in Shalley Park. Then, when you get home from school, we will leave for camp. I suggest that you pack tonight. We need to get into the field as soon as possible. We can stay two nights out there."

Bergita shook her head. "I think one night is more than enough. If you want to stay longer, Claudette, that's up to you, but I don't want the children missing church on Sunday for this."

Claudette scowled but didn't argue.

Bergita patted Ava's shoulder before she walked back behind the counter. "Ava, if your mother would rather you came the next morning, that will be fine," Bergita said. "I could meet you in the parking lot if Claudette already has Colin and Andi out searching for birds."

A horn honked outside. Ava's hour was up.

Ava gathered up her backpack. "That's my brother. I have to go. I'll see you at school tomorrow." She nodded at Colin and me.

Colin and I followed her out of the house.

"Don't forget to ask your mom about camping tomorrow night," I said as she opened the front door.

She glanced over her shoulder and a strange look crossed over face, almost as though she was in pain.

"Are you okay, Ava?" Colin asked. He must have noticed her expression too.

She forced a smile. "I'm fine. Why wouldn't I be? We're going to ace this project and then we can go back to not liking each other." She went through the door.

When we walked down the porch steps, I was surprised to see my sister outside the house. She stood a few feet away from Ava's brother, who was leaning on the hood of his truck. His black hair was wet and slicked back as if he had just washed it, and he had a lazy smile as he spoke to Bethany. Something he said made her laugh. I hadn't heard her laugh like that since her best friend Kaylee from our old neighborhood visited a few weeks ago.

I hurried over to them. "Bethany, what are you doing?" The question popped out of my mouth.

Bethany scowled. "Geez, Andi, what's the problem? I'm talking to Ava's brother while we waited for you kids to come outside. Romero and I know each other from school."

Romero smiled. "That's right. Beth and I have the same study hall. It's the best fifty minutes of the day."

Beth? No one calls Bethany, Beth.

"Romero, let's go," Ava said climbing into the truck. She refused to look at us.

Romero pushed himself off the truck hood and smiled one last time. "See you in study hall, Beth."

Bethany blushed. My sister actually blushed.

He got in the truck and drove down the street.

I dug my fists into my hips just like Claudette had done earlier that afternoon.

Colin looked from Bethany to me and back again, before running into the house. "I'll go talk to Claudette and Bergita about the camp out," he called.

I didn't even bother to respond. All of my energy was focused on my sister. "What are you doing talking to Romero? How do you know him?"

She pulled her long blonde hair back into a pony-tail and secured it with a band from her wrist. "He just told you we have the same study hall. He's a sophomore at my school. Relax, Andi. What's your problem?"

"How can he have a car if he's a sophomore?"

She rolled her eyes. "He turned sixteen the first week of school, that's how."

I crossed my arms. "He's Ava's brother. Ava, who hates me. He's *her* brother."

She rolled her eyes. "Just because he's Ava's brother, and you and Ava don't get along, doesn't mean I can't talk to him. I thought you and Amelie wanted me to make friends in Killdeer. You're always nagging me about it."

I dropped my arms. "We do. It's just," I paused. "I don't know why, I think he's trouble. He looks like trouble to me."

Bethany's face flushed. "All I was doing was talking to him. Chill out. And your opinion of which boys I talk to or don't talk to doesn't matter. You aren't my mother. Mine's dead, remember? And so is yours." She spun around and stomped back to our house. She slammed the door so hard that the fall wreath Amelie had hanging on it fell off.

During science the next day at school, I wanted to go over our plan for camping and birding with Colin and Ava. Ava had emailed Colin and me late the night before saying she could come to the bird campout. Bergita and Claudette were at Shalley Park that very moment, scouting out the best places to look for the elusive Kirtland's warbler.

There was just one problem. Ava wasn't in school all day.

When Colin and I got home from school, I hopped off my bike. "How could Ava be gone today of all days? It's our only chance to talk about the project before the campout tonight. What if she doesn't come?"

Colin frowned. "Maybe she's sick."

"If she's sick she can't go camping. Then what are we going to do?"

Colin sighed. "We'd better call her and find out. Claudette's going to want to leave as soon as possible." Colin handed me his cell phone.

"You want me to call her?"

He grinned.

I rolled my eyes and dialed the number Ava had given me yesterday.

"Hello?" a male voice asked.

"Hi, this is Andi. Is Ava there?"

"She's not here," the guy said and hung up. It had to be Romero.

I stared at Colin's cell phone. "I think her brother just hung up on me."

Colin opened his mouth, but before he could say anymore, Ava came up the sidewalk. A pack was strapped to her back, and Bergita's binoculars dangled from her neck. "What are you two doing standing out here? I thought you'd be helping Bergita pack her granola or whatever she plans to feed us on this campout."

"You weren't in school today," I accused.

She dropped her pack in the grass. "Are you in charge of taking attendance now?"

"We were going to plan out the trip during science."

"We can do it tonight. We'll be trapped in a tent together for hours, won't we?"

"You could have told us if you planned to miss school. We were afraid you weren't going to show up."

"If I say I'm going to be somewhere, I'm going to be there. Don't worry your pink little head about it."

I touched my hair self-consciously.

The screen door to my house opened, and my aunt Amelie ran down the porch stairs. She was barefoot and the skirt of her flowered maxi dress brushed the tops of her toes. All she needed was a ring of daisies in her hair to finish the free spirit look. She was only twenty-six. She was young, especially for having one child in high school and one in middle school.

"Ava," Amelie said. "It's so nice to finally meet you."

Ava narrowed her eyes as if she wondered what I had told Amelie about her.

"I hope you kids have fun." My aunt grinned. "And try to keep Bergita and her sister out of trouble. I just met Claudette a little while ago. She's a trip. I don't think I have the bail money to cover all of you." She placed a hand on my shoulder. "Andi, can I talk to you a minute?"

She led me a few feet away and sighed. "I know you will be fine with Bergita, but I can't help being nervous. It's the first night you've spent away from home since you and Bethany moved here."

"It's only one night, and Bethany has spent a night away at her friends' back home," I said.

"True, and I was just a nervous wreck about that too. This parenting thing is way harder than I expected it to be. I worry about you girls all the time."

I hugged her. "We worry about you too."

I felt her smile against the top of my head. "I love you." She stood and brushed at her eyes. "Bethany and I will hold down the fort while you're gone."

"What are you going to do?" I asked.

"I promised your sister a trip to the mall in Canton tomorrow. She's inside making a list of all the stores we're going to hit. My feet are already tired. Do you need me to pick you up anything while we're out shopping?"

I shook my head. I had enough jeans and T-shirts to get through the week. I didn't need much more than that when it came to clothes. "Did she say anything about a new friend?"

My aunt clasped her hands in front of her chest. "A new friend? No! Bethany made a friend at school?"

"I think so," I said.

"Maybe we can invite her shopping too," Amelie said, grinning ear to ear. "I've been praying for this so hard."

I didn't think Romero was the answer my aunt had been praying for, but I didn't correct her and tell her the *her* she was referring to was actually a *him*. If Amelie was having trouble parenting us through camping trips, who knew how she would handle Bethany and boys.

Claudette walked out of the Carters' house carrying a small cooler in one hand and her phone in the other. "Saddle up, cowpokes. Birds wait for no one. I just saw a post online. A Mississippi kite was spotted near where we're camping tonight. That will be a great start to your lists. They are pretty hard to spot around these parts too. Not as rare as a Kirtland's but noteworthy."

Claudette dropped her phone into the breast pocket of her shirt. She was wearing what I would call safari chic: a tan safari hat, shirt, and shorts. Despite her age, her legs were muscular. I bet she could hike for fifty miles at a stretch. I would be lucky to last five.

"Have a good time," Amelie said. "And be careful."

I gave Amelie a final hug, and Bethany stepped outside our house. She frowned at me. I wasn't sure if she was more upset about our fight yesterday or the fact that Romero didn't drop Ava off (which meant she didn't get to flirt with him again).

I took a deep breath and ran over to my sister. Before she could stop me, I gave her hug. "Bye," I said. "I love you." Ever since my parents died, I knew that saying a proper good-bye was important. Sometimes you didn't get a second chance to say it.

Her face softened. "Have fun at bird geek camp." It was her way of saying I love you in return.

I ran to the car and climbed into the back of Bergita's station wagon, which was already packed.

Ava sat across from me, forcing Colin into the middle seat with all of the gear.

Bergita slammed the door after us.

Ava buckled her seatbelt. "Your aunt offers to buy you something, just like that. She takes your sister on a shopping spree? It must be nice."

"It won't be a shopping spree," I said. "Bethany might get a couple of new things, but not everything that she wants, trust me."

Ava folded her arms. "Oh, thanks for clearing that up. To some of us two things from the mall is a shopping spree."

I tried to ignore her. With a little pang in my chest,

I stared out the window. Amelie waved, and even Bethany wiggled her fingers. I waved back as we drove away and couldn't help but remember waving to my parents before they left on that last trip.

In the small gravel parking lot just outside Killdeer's forest, we shouldered our packs.
Claudette heaved on a backpack twice the size of anyone else's.

"We have to hurry," she said. "We want to make
camp fast so we can get some birding in tonight. The
best time for birding is dawn. Near sunset is decent too,
when the birds are tucking in for the night. We might
have a chance to get an hour of scouting in before dark.
If we're lucky, we might even see a barred owl."

"Don't you need permission or a permit to camp in
the woods?" Colin asked.

Bergita laughed. "I'm surprised you haven't asked
before, Colin. We have a permit. There's nothing to
worry about. We aren't breaking any rules."

"Oh," he said, blushing.

"No more small talk. Time to hit the trail." Claudette grabbed both straps of her pack and headed into the forest.

Bergita winked. "Claudette is an excellent birder even if she is a little" — she searched for the right word — "intense." She was the second relative to describe Claudette that way.

We followed Claudette across the tree line, and we had only walked three feet when she barked in a hoarse whisper, "Two o'clock." Even though she was whispering, it sounded like she was shouting in the stillness of the forest.

"What?" I asked, looking at my watch. It was almost five. Nowhere near two o'clock.

"There is a gray flycatcher at two o'clock." She pointed in a semi-circle. "I hope you understand how to read an analog clock. That's how we'll identify the directions to look."

"I don't see anything," Colin whispered even though he was looking in the right direction.

"Use your binoculars. That's what they're for," Claudette ordered.

The three of us kids held our binoculars up to our eyes. I turned to two o'clock and saw fuzzy trees. I focused the lenses, and a tiny bird, not much bigger than a hummingbird, came into focus. How Claudette spotted the bird that far away I would never know. She really was a super birder.

Bergita snapped some pictures with her massive

camera, and Colin made a note in our project notebook. Bird one: check. We were going to ace this assignment.

"That was so cool," I said.

Claudette shared a rare grin. "That's just the beginning. You kids are in for the time of your lives!"

"Somehow I doubt that," Ava muttered behind me.

Claudette resumed the march. Every so often we would stop. Claudette would hear something no one else could hear and play a bird song back on her phone. Most of the time, a bird appeared at her call like magic. It was almost as though she was the Pied Piper for anything with feathers.

We were almost an hour into the hike and Claudette was frozen in front of us playing a palm warbler song. According to the map, the campsite was only a mile from the parking lot, but we stopped every few paces for Claudette to listen to the woods. The palm warbler never appeared and she started moving again.

Ava poked me with a stick from the forest floor. "Do you see something or are you blocking traffic?"

I glared at her and stepped out of the way.

The trees broke into a clearing. There were people with binoculars hanging from their necks setting up campsites. At least a half dozen tents were going up.

On the south end of the clearing, there was a crumbling stone building. I guessed it was the haunted Shalley homestead.

Bergita caught me staring at the ruins. "That house is nearly two hundred years old. Before this was a park, the land belonged to the Shalley family. I don't think anyone has lived on it for at least a hundred years. The story goes that there were five sons in the family and every last one of them died during the Civil War: one in active combat, the other four from disease. Twenty-some years ago, a descendent of the family who lives in another state donated the land to the city and asked that it be turned into a park in the city's honor."

"All five sons died?" I asked barely above a whisper.

She nodded. "The Civil War had more American casualties than any war before or since."

"That's terrible." I continued to stare at the crumbling house. "But why didn't someone try to save the house?"

Bergita sighed. "It would have been a nice old house to save, but by the time the town got ownership of the land, it was too far gone. I'm glad they decided not to tear it down all the way. It's a nice tribute to the family that it's still there. Now nature can reclaim it in her own old sweet time."

"Is that all that's left of the family?" Ava asked.

I glanced at her in surprise. I had been so engrossed in Bergita's story I hadn't noticed Ava.

Bergita shook her head. "All five boys are buried a little ways along the path." She pointed at a break in the trees near the south wall of the house. "The family had a private cemetery, but the boys are the only ones buried there."

"I thought the ghost was a woman," I said.

Bergita patted my shoulder. "Oh, don't pay any mind to that silly story."

Claudette marched toward us. "It's time to set up

camp." She pointed across the campground. "We'll camp over there. I don't sleep next to crumbling old houses that are probably full of all sorts of critters. It's a motto I live by."

We followed Bergita and Claudette to the far end of the field. It was over a ridge. From where we camped, I could see the upper edge of the house's crumbling wall, but the rest of it was hidden.

We dropped our packs where Claudette directed. "Have any of you pitched a tent before?"

The three of us kids shared a look.

"Why am I not surprised?" Claudette grumbled. "Kids are happier today sitting inside and playing on the computer instead of getting outside and in touch with nature like they should be. It's disgraceful. Completely disgraceful, if you ask me."

"I know how to pitch a tent," I said, hoping it was true. "I used to camp in the backyard with my dad all the time when I was little."

"Maybe the next generation isn't a complete loss. Get started," Claudette ordered.

I untied the tent bags and dumped the contents in the grass, wincing. There were about a thousand pieces for the tent Ava and I were going to share.

Colin unzipped his pup tent, and it sprang to life. All he had to do was pound its stakes into the ground so that it wouldn't blow away. I wished our tent was that simple.

"Do you really know how to put that thing together?" Ava asked.

"Sure." I picked up one of the metal sticks. "How

hard can it be?" I started pushing a rod through the loops in the fabric.

A man with a round belly was walking by and said, "That piece is for the roof. You just stuck it in the hole for the door."

I blushed and pulled the rod out of the fabric. "Oh, right."

Ava groaned.

"Any time." He grinned. "It's nice to see kids taking an interest in birding."

Colin drove the last stake for his tent into the ground. "We're here to look for the Kirtland's warbler."

The man nodded. "We all are." He held out his hand. "I'm Gregory Sparrow."

Ava arched an eyebrow. "Your last name is Sparrow, and you're a birder?"

He laughed. "I suppose I was destined to be a birder with that name."

Claudette marched toward us, her arms loaded with firewood. I was beginning to realize that marching was her favorite way to get around. "Gregory, what are you doing over here? Don't you have a bird to misidentify on your side of the campground?"

His grin faltered. "I've never had a misidentification in my life. That can't be said for everyone here." He gave her a pointed look. "Now, can it?"

Claudette dropped her stack of wood onto the ground. "You won't get any information from these kids."

He put a hand to his chest. "Claudette, I'm offended that you would think I would have an ulterior motive to be friendly. I was greeting your camp mates here." The man looked at the three of us. "I haven't been formally introduced to your companions."

Bergita joined us. "Colin is my grandson, Gregory." She set her hand on Colin's shoulder.

He smiled. "I should have known they were here because of you, Bergita. Claudette doesn't have a maternal bone in her body." The corners of Gregory's mouth turned up. "I hope they don't slow you down, Claud. It would be a shame if I spotted the Kirtland's and you missed it, wouldn't it?"

"It's more likely to be the other way around. I've out-birded you the last three locations. Don't forget that," Claudette said.

Ava, Colin, and I shared a look.

Gregory's eyes fell on Ava and he smiled. "Aren't you Fiorella's daughter?"

Ava's tan skin paled.

"I thought you were. Shame she can't clean for us anymore. My wife's still lamenting the fact she stopped working. She claimed that Fiorella was the best maid ever. Apparently, the new help my wife found isn't measuring up."

Just as quickly as the color drained from Ava's face, her complexion flushed. "Don't talk about my mother."

He raised his eyebrows. "I was being complimentary. I didn't mean anything by it."

"Don't talk about my mother," Ava hissed.

Gregory frowned but said nothing more about it.

Bergita shielded her eyes in the direction of

Gregory's camp. "Gregory, I see one of your students waving. You had better go check what he needs."

He looked behind him. Everyone at his camp was quietly setting up. It was a group of four college students. Two girls and two boys. Susan was the only student I knew. She had been one of the camp counselors at Discovery Camp that Colin, Ava, and I went to at the university that summer. She waved at us.

Gregory said good-bye and returned to his camp.

"Did you lie?" I asked Bergita. "I don't see anyone from his camp waving at him."

Bergita winked. "No, one of the students was waving. I didn't say she was waving *at* Gregory."

"Who is he?" Colin asked.

"A windbag," Claudette complained. "He thinks he's an expert when it comes to birds. I'm the expert. All his book learning can't match what I have seen in the field."

Bergita knelt and unrolled her sleeping bag. "He's a biology professor, I think. He teaches ornithology. That's how he and Claudette know each other."

"I thought all the science professors were at Discovery Camp this summer," I said.

Bergita shook her head. "You met only a few. Michael Pike has a large faculty for its size."

Claudette grunted.

"I didn't know there would be other birders camping out," I said.

"Of course, there will be," Claudette practically growled. "If there is a sighting as coveted as a Kirtland's, birders will come from all over the state.

There will be even more birders in the woods come morning. The wimps stay in a motel. Those truly committed to the cause, camp."

"Oh, umm, okay." I stepped back.

"Let's finish putting up the tent," Ava said. For once, I agreed with her.

After we set up camp, Claudette took us on what could only be described as a death march. The blisters on my feet had blisters. I couldn't remember the last time I had been so tired. The three of us kids limped behind Claudette and Bergita as we trekked through the woods. Bergita shuffled along too, but her sister marched on as though she was ready to attack the Appalachian Trail.

Bergita called up to her sister at the front of our line. "Claud, I think it's time to head back to camp. It's starting to get dark, and the kids need their rest. We won't be able to walk a mile tomorrow if you tire us out tonight."

"Scarlet Tanager, one o'clock." Claudette had her binoculars pointed high in the trees.

Bergita sighed but dutifully lifted her own binoculars to her eyes.

The bird was bright red and beautiful. I let the binoculars hang from my neck in order to log the sighting in our assignment notebook. Since we arrived, we had seen ten varieties of birds. There was no chance that any other group in our class would see more. The ten extra credit points were a lock. The additional twenty points depended on the Kirtland's warbler. That bird was still missing in action.

I slid the pen into the spiral bind of the notebook and lifted my binoculars to my eyes again. Everyone was still watching the tanager. I searched the trees for something new. Secretly, I hoped I would be the one who spotted the Kirtland's for the first time. It would drive Ava crazy to know I found it before she did. I swept my gaze through the trees, both high and low. Different birds moved in different levels of the forest. Some, like tanagers, liked to be high up, and others, like thrushes, liked to be close to the ground.

When I moved my gaze lower, I spotted a dot of red in the brush. I focused in on the color and saw it was a cardinal. We had seen at least half a dozen of Ohio's state bird during the hike. It wasn't so much the bird that caught my interest, but what he was perched on. It was a stone, a large polished stone.

I took a few steps to the right for a better angle. There was a faint engraving in the stone. It was faded but legible. "S-h-a," I read aloud.

Ava lowered her binoculars. "What are you looking at?"

"I think it's the Shalley's cemetery," I said.

"Let's go check it out," Ava said and stepped off the path.

"Wait," I said. "Claudette wouldn't like that. She said from the start we have to follow her."

She snorted. "Claudette is going to be looking at that tanager for the next twenty minutes. Come on. Unless you're scared of the ghost."

I gritted my teeth and followed her off the path.

There were five headstones in the graveyard, one for each Shalley son who died during the Civil War. Moss grew around the base of each stone and ivy climbed up the sides. The once sharp edges of the names chiseled in the granite were worn by a century and a half of rain, wind, and snow. To my surprise, a small potted mum sat at the head of each grave. The cardinal flew from the headstone to a neighboring sycamore tree.

I knelt in front of the first grave marker. "RIP. William A. Shalley. Beloved son. December 1, 1840-July 4, 1863. Battle of Gettysburg."

"I wonder who put the flowers here," I said.

Ava shrugged.

I went to each grave and read the names, "Harold, Randall, Matthew, and Luke. Don't you think it's odd that all the graves are men, but the ghost is supposed to be a woman? Who is she?"

Ava walked to the far end of the cemetery. "Whoa!"

"What is it?" I jumped up.

She pointed down. I walked over to her and pulled up short. My toes hung over the edge of a deep ravine that was masked by a wall of trees. "Yikes. We should be careful."

"Yeah, I don't want to fall down there. Did you see those rocks at the bottom?"

I swallowed.

Bergita broke through the trees. "Did you girls see a bird back here?"

Ava and I spun around.

Bergita put a hand to her mouth. "Good heavens, this is the Shalley cemetery." She stepped over William's grave. "You know, I've lived in Killdeer my entire life and have never seen them."

"Bergita," I asked, bending down and touching one of the burgundy blossoms on Harold's grave. "Do you know who put the flowers on the graves?"

She examined the closest mum. "It would be Patrick Finnigan, I would guess."

"Mr. Finnigan?" I asked.

"Why would the town curator put flowers on the graves?" Ava asked.

"It's part of his job." She ran a yellow bandana across her forehead. "Since he deals with all things historical in Killdeer, he has to do it. One of the stipulations of the city getting the land, I believe, is the graveyard has to be protected. You see, the grass is mowed around the stones too, don't you?"

Now that she mentioned it, I did see the grass had been recently cut, but it was hard for me to imagine lanky Mr. Finnigan bringing a mower into the woods while wearing his bow tie and sports jacket.

In any case, it sounded like Colin and I needed to visit Mr. Finnigan's museum inside the old bottling company again.

"He might want to work on keeping the headstones clean," Ava said. "They are covered in moss and ivy."

Bergita laughed. "I'll be sure to tell him the next time I see him. But let's get going. Right now, Claudette is distracted by an Eastern Towhee, but before she heard the towhee, she agreed to head back to camp. I hope you girls like hot dogs, baked beans, and s'mores because that's what is on the dinner menu. It's real campout food."

I took one last look around the cemetery. Grass, weeds, and fallen leaves covered the graves, but then I noticed something different about the far grave — Matthew's grave. I walked over to it. On a small patch of earth there wasn't any grass or weeds, just fresh dirt. "It looks like something has been digging here," I said.

Bergita stood next to me. "We're in the middle of the woods. There are all sorts of critters that can dig a hole like that. Rabbits, chipmunks, raccoons, and even skunks."

I squatted by the spot. "It doesn't look like an animal did this. See, the patch makes a perfect square. What rabbit or raccoon would dig in a straight line like that?" I pointed. "And look at this. I think I see a partial print of a shoe. Like someone stomped down the ground after he was done digging."

Bergita tapped her chin thoughtfully. "Maybe Mr. Finnigan took a piece of ground back for the historical society to preserve in the museum. He is always collecting odds and ends from town and putting them inside his museum."

Ava stood above me now too. "He puts dirt in the museum?"

"It's historic dirt," Bergita said with a shrug. "We'd better go before Claudette changes her mind about letting us return to camp because she wants to see just one more bird. I don't know about you, but I'm exhausted. I know my sister—there is always just one more bird to see. The woman is crazy, but I can't help but love her."

When we stepped through the trees and back on the path, Colin and Claudette were right where we left them. Both had their binoculars trained on a towhee barely visible in the deep brush.

"Do you see the burnt orange color under his wing? Simply gorgeous," Claudette gushed. "I've seen these beauties dozens of times, but it never gets old. I love them."

"It's getting dark, Claudette," Bergita hinted.

The supreme birder sighed. "I suppose we should head back."

"We did great though," Colin said. "Twelve species today. That's amazing."

Claudette shared a rare grin. "That's just the beginning, my boy. Tomorrow will be even better."

As we left the woods, I couldn't help looking over my shoulder to where I knew the cemetery was hidden by the trees. I didn't believe Mr. Finnigan dug that hole and took a dirt sample for the museum. Something about that patch of dirt bothered me. I suspected there was a much creepier reason why it was there that may or may not involve a real ghost.

As soon as we returned to camp, Bergita and Claudette put us to work setting up the campfire and cooking hot dogs for dinner. Bergita brought enough food to the campground for a small army, so she invited all the other birders camping out to our area to eat. They brought over their lawn chairs and created a huge circle around the campfire. There must have been thirty people there in all. Even Gregory and his students came over.

Susan punched me in the arm as a greeting.

"Ow," I muttered rubbing the spot with my free hand. My other hand held a stick with three skewered hot dogs over the fire.

The university's star softball player chuckled. "It's nice to see you kids again. I'm not a bit surprised that you're out here looking for the Kirtland's. Dr. Sparrow said Claudette was your aunt, Colin."

Colin wiped mustard from his cheek with the back of his hand. "That's right."

"That's awesome. She's one of the most famous birders out there, and I've read a ton of articles about her. She's been all over the world. From what I've read, she'll go to any length to see a bird. I'd write a paper about her for this class if Dr. Sparrow didn't hate her so much." Susan grimaced. "Sorry, Colin."

"Why doesn't he like her?" I asked.

Susan shrugged as she waved at the other students. "Guys, come here."

The three other college students joined us. "This is Paige, Campbell, and Spooner. Guys, these are the kids from Discovery Camp I was telling you about."

Campbell was a tall guy with a long face and glasses. "So you're the kids that solved the mystery of the chem lab last summer." He gave Colin a fist bump. "Nice work."

Colin blushed. "Thanks. Are you guys here for a class then?"

Susan nodded. "Yeah, we're all in ornithology. It's pretty awesome that a Kirtland's warbler is in town the same time we're taking the class."

Everyone except Paige agreed. She watched the woods and chewed on her lip.

"Earth to Paige," Spooner, a huge guy with cheeks like a chipmunk's, said. "What are you staring at?"

She shook her head, and her dark bobbed hair bounced back and forth. "Nothing."

"She's worried about the ghost," Susan said in a conspiratorial whisper.

Paige scowled. "That's not it," she said, but her voice quavered just a little.

"Did someone say something about a ghost?" a voice asked.

"I believe I heard it too, Brother Joe," a second identical voice said.

"As did I, Brother Jack," a third voice said.

Across the fire pit three elderly men sat in identical lawn chairs, wearing identical gray striped T-shirts, jeans, and white tennis shoes.

"The Higgins triplets. Jim, Joe, and Jack," Susan muttered. "I should have known they would be here."

I removed the cooked hot dogs from my stick and placed them on a platter on a small, folding tray table next to me. Claudette had carried the table in her pack along with everything else. "Why?"

"They come to all the birder things too."

"Do you know the story?" another birder asked the triplets. "I've never heard it start to finish."

"That's a shame," one of the triplets said.

"That it is," another agreed.

"We must tell it," the third said.

Behind him, the last of the sun's rays dipped below the treetops, leaving behind a purple, blue, and gray bruised sky.

Claudette gripped a plastic cup in her lawn chair. "There is no ghost of Shalley Park. As naturalists, we shouldn't perpetuate that nonsense."

"Oh, Claudette," Gregory said from the far side

of the campfire. "What's a campout without a good old-fashioned ghost story?" He raised a thick eyebrow at her as if in challenge.

She glared at him over the firelight but said nothing more.

This was a story I wanted to hear. Colin, Ava, and I sat on the grass near Bergita's feet. I stuck a line of four marshmallows on my stick and placed it back over the fire.

"Who should tell the tale?" a triplet asked.

"Why don't you do it, Jim? You share it with such gusto," one of his brothers said.

Jim, the triplet in the middle, nodded. The side conversations died down as the other birders settled around the fire with their hot dogs and s'mores to listen.

"Never underestimate the power of a mother's love," Jim began. "Because that is what this story is about: about a mother who lost everything she held dear for a country she didn't even know," he added in a low voice.

We all leaned as close as we dared to the fire.

"Dominika Shalley was born in Russia near about 1800 to a poor Gypsy family. She and her family moved many times around Eastern Europe. The gypsies were never truly welcome, you see. No European nation wanted them, so they moved often to escape persecution. Dominika did not like the nomadic life of her people and longed for a place to call home.

"Silas Shalley was in Vienna studying architecture.

He came from a wealthy family in New York and had great plans for his future. While Dominika searched for a home, he searched for adventure. The pair met when Dominika attempted to steal Silas's wallet on the steps of St. Stephen's Cathedral. It was love at first sight for Silas, and for Dominika, it was a chance to escape a life she hated.

"They married shortly thereafter, and Silas brought his wife back to New York. His rich family was not pleased their son married a gypsy, so Silas used what money he had to buy land as far away from his parents as he could afford, which brought him here to Killdeer, Ohio. For Silas, it was a new adventure. For Dominika, it was again an escape, this time from her husband's disapproving relatives."

Jim waved his hands around. "Here they lived and raised their boys. For the first time, Dominika had a home and happiness. However, when her oldest son was twenty-one, the South left the Union. All five of her boys went off to war. She begged them not to go. Dominika had no interest in preserving the Union, and she didn't care what the Southern states she had never seen did. However, the boys were like their father and sought adventure. The youngest, William, went off to war as soon as he turned sixteen, in 1862. Each boy who left met a cruel fate."

Jim took a breath and examined the faces staring at him through the fire. "Randall and Matthew were the first to perish. They died in 1861 in the camps outside of Washington. Both men died of pneumonia. Then,

Harold died in January 1862 from a bullet wound that led to gangrene. And Luke died of infection when his leg was amputated."

Beside me, Ava took in a quick breath. I chewed on my lip as I imagined the stone house behind the triplets standing upright and with a candle in every window for the boys who never returned. I could almost see Dominika Shalley in the doorway, holding another letter telling her another son had died.

Jim continued, "Each time Silas and Dominika received word of another son's death, Dominika went into hysterics. She blamed Silas for what had happened. She thought he could have done more to discourage the boys from going off to war. Then in 1863, the greatest blow came. William, her youngest and favorite son, died when he was killed defending Little Round Top at Gettysburg. He was shot in the head."

I shivered.

"After that, Dominika became hysterical and stayed hysterical. Her husband didn't know what to do. Finally, two years after the war ended, he decided to take her back to New York for treatment, but they never made it. The night before they were set to leave, Dominika died in her bed." He paused. "From a broken heart.

"After his wife died, Silas abandoned the home and fled to California. He never returned, but Dominika did." Jim leaned closer to the fire, so that it illuminated the planes of his face and dipped his eyes in shadow. "She walks the woods every night to visit the graves of her boys. You can hear her crying. Some have even reported seeing her in a white robe and long silver hair trailing behind her. Her feet hovering above the earth."

"Hogwash," Claudette said, as if she couldn't take it anymore. "It's a silly story to keep children out of the woods. I don't believe a word of it."

Jim wiggled his eyebrows before leaning back into his chair. "Just because you don't believe it doesn't mean it's untrue."

Claudette snorted.

Trying to cover the creepy feeling climbing up my neck, I removed the marshmallows from the fire and blew out the flame caught on the stick. With one hand, I made a sandwich of graham cracker and chocolate and squished the marshmallow into the sandwich.

Bergita flipped her braid over her shoulder as she thrust her marshmallow stick into the flames. "That's a good story, Jim. Wonderful performance."

Across the fire, the triplets chuckled together.

I handed the s'more to Colin and started to construct another.

"Do you believe that story?" he whispered.

"Of course not," I said, but my voice shook just a little.

Ava snorted and grabbed the stick from me. She took the last marshmallow. "It's a dumb story about a crazy lady."

"I don't think it's dumb," I said, feeling the need to defend Dominika. "I think it's sad."

Ava examined me over her s'more. "So you believe there's a ghost that haunts these woods at night?"

I scowled and scooted closer to Colin, nearly knocking him off the log. "I didn't say that. I feel bad for Dominika is all."

She rolled her eyes before facing the fire. "You feel bad for someone who died over one hundred and fifty years ago. There are plenty of people to feel sorry for today."

I wondered what she meant by that, but I was afraid to ask. I stood and Colin followed me. "The only way we're going to know if that story is true is to find out for ourselves."

"Mr. Finnigan will know," Colin agreed.

I flipped up the hood of my sweatshirt. "I have the casebook in my pack."

"You brought the casebook? Why?" Colin whispered.

"I thought we might need it."

"Do you think Dominika's ghost is a case?"

I twisted my mouth in thought. "There's something else. I think someone is digging up the Shalley boys' graves."

"What?" Colin yelped.

I clamped a hand over his mouth. Luckily, no one around the camp looked in our direction. I lowered my hand. "Shhh."

Claudette muttered to herself.

"What's that, Claudette?" Gregory called. "We can't hear you."

"I don't think it was right for Jim to tell that story right before the children are going to sleep. They could have nightmares."

"Children?" Gregory asked. "I don't see any children here, just young people, but certainly not children." He sat back in his chair.

Claudette grunted. "In any case, I don't think it's right to share a false story."

"False? How can you be so sure?" Gregory asked.

She glared back at him. "You believe it?"

Gregory grinned. "Maybe your night in the camp tonight will make you a believer. Never doubt the power of a mother's love, as Jim said."

I noticed he didn't answer Claudette's question.

Bergita zipped up her coat. "Okay, I think that's enough ghost stories for one night. You kids hit the hay."

Claudette polished off the last of her s'more and gave Gregory one final glare. "Yes, that's true. I'll be kicking you out of your tents at five."

"Five?" Ava yelped. "The sun's not even up then."

Claudette wiped chocolate from her cheek with the back of hand. "We need to be in position for optimal birding."

Gregory grinned through the fire. "The early birder gets the bird."

Bergita herded Colin, Ava, and me toward our tents.

I slowed my pace. "Bergita, what's the deal with Gregory and Claudette?"

"Deal?" She glanced over her shoulder. "What deal? There's no deal." She said this like she was nervous about something, and she kept looking at her sister.

There was definitely a deal.

Before we climbed into our tents, I tugged on Colin's sleeve. "Meet me outside your tent at midnight."

"Andi, I don't know ..."

"Just do it, okay?"

"Okay." He nodded and disappeared inside his tent.

I grabbed my toothbrush and toothpaste from my tent and walked to the washhouse. At least our campsite had running water and a real bathroom.

I started to push in the bathroom door but stopped when I heard voices.

"Paige, come on, it's just a story. It's not true," I heard Susan say.

"How do we know?" Paige replied. "What if the ghost comes and haunts us? Her house is just yards from where we're sleeping."

"You're being ridiculous."

"You won't think that if you're attacked by a ghost."

Susan started to laugh uncontrollably.

"Hey," Paige said. "It's not funny."

"Oh, come on, it's a little funny."

Paige giggled. "Maybe."

"Let's go to the tent. It'll be safer to be in the tent than out in the open when the ghost comes. Bwahaha!"

Paige snorted a laugh.

I jumped back from the door and ducked around the side of the washhouse. When I could no longer hear the girls' laughter, I went inside to brush my teeth. By the time I returned to the tent, Ava was already in her sleeping bag. She lay on her side and pretended to be asleep. That was fine with me.

I crawled into my own sleeping bag and tried to stay awake. It was almost nine o'clock and pitch black outside except for the glow of the dying fire. I could hear the low murmur of some of the birders who were still up. I only had to stay awake for three hours. I yawned.

I jerked awake. Did I oversleep? Did I miss my meeting with Colin? I ducked deeper into my sleeping bag to find my flashlight and my watch. It said eleven fifty. Phew. I didn't sleep too late.

Ava's breathing was deeper than it had been when I crawled into the tent. She was really asleep now, but I had better check to be sure. "Ava?" I whispered. Nothing. Outside, the chatter around the campfire had stopped. I sat up in my sleeping bag. As quietly as possible, I slipped out of the bag and crawled to the front of the tent. I tugged on the zipper. With every pull, it made a screeching sound, and I winced. I glanced back at Ava. She didn't move.

Finally, the opening in the tent was big enough for me to slip through. I tossed my shoes out of the opening. Outside the tent, I gripped my flashlight in my hand, but I didn't switch it on. The firepit held glowing embers, but the birders were asleep. Colin's tent was on the other side of Claudette's. I would have to be extra careful when walking by his aunt. I suspected that Claudette was a light sleeper. Her ears were always perked to hear a bird.

I slipped on my shoes and crept around the back of Claudette's tent. Colin wasn't out in front of it. "Colin," I whispered.

I didn't hear anything.

I tapped on the side of his tent. "Colin?" I tapped the side of the tent a second time.

"What? What?" Colin flailed inside his tent.

"Shh. It's Andi!" I hissed, looking around the campground to see if the noise woke anyone up. Nothing moved except inside Colin's tent.

A few seconds later, Colin crawled out of his tent. He wasn't wearing shoes, and his glasses sat crookedly on his nose. He stood up and fixed his glasses then reached into the tent for his shoes.

"Let's go," I whispered. Colin ducked back into his tent one more time and came out with his flashlight. "You haven't told me what's going on."

"I'll tell you when we're in the woods. We might be overheard here. Don't turn on your flashlight until I say so."

Colin followed me without question into the trees. For a second, I felt disoriented. In the dark, the trail looked so much different than it had during the daylight.

Colin pulled on the sleeve of my sweatshirt. "Where are we going? Can you tell me now?"

"Remember where we saw the scarlet tanager?" I asked as I started down the path.

In the dark, I saw Colin's head move in a nod. "Sure."

"Do you know the way back there? I want to show you something."

"Can I turn on my flashlight? I won't be able to get back there if I can't see where I'm going."

"Okay, I think we're far enough away from camp now."

He flicked on his flashlight and aimed the beam onto the path. "This is the way. Can you tell me why we're going back there in the middle of the night?"

"While you and Claudette were looking at the scarlet tanager, Ava and I found the Shalleys' cemetery and the graves of the five Shalley boys killed during the Civil War."

"You and Ava did something together? Voluntarily?"

"Well, I found it, and Ava insisted that we check it out."

Colin stopped in the middle of the path and shone the flashlight just below my chin. "Why didn't you tell me about it then?"

I held up my hand. "Bergita was in a hurry to get back to camp. I didn't get a chance. Can you lower your light?"

Colin lowered his flashlight but not before I saw the look of hurt cross his face. "We saw the tanager right up here."

I turned on my flashlight and was about to point the beam into the woods where I knew the graveyard would be, but movement and a glint of floating light stopped me. Someone else was in the woods. I grabbed Colin's flashlight from his hand and turned it off.

"Wha—"

I covered his mouth with my hand.

Colin pulled my hand away from his mouth. "What's going on?" he whispered. "I wish you'd stop doing that."

I pointed into the trees where the light was. Colin and I inched over in that direction. I placed a finger to my lips. He nodded. We crept half bent over, so that no part of us showed over the thick bushes. Through the dark branches, I saw a white form float through the trees on the other side of the cemetery beyond the ravine.

"Holy smokes," Colin yelped.

The form moved on and disappeared deep into the woods. I wished I had thought to bring my binoculars. I didn't think I would need them at night.

Colin and I sat together crouched for a few minutes holding each other's hands. I gripped his hands so tightly I was surprised they didn't break. Finally, I let go and straightened up.

Colin grabbed my arm and breathed. "Did you see that?"

I knew what he meant, but I was reluctant to

answer. I felt like if I answered that would make what I saw real, and I *really* didn't want that to be the case.

"Let's go back to the campground," Colin whispered.

"We have to at least look at the graves. We came all this way." I straightened my shoulders.

Colin sighed.

I turned on my flashlight and pushed through the brush to the cemetery. I shone my light on the graves. In addition to the disturbed dirt on Matthew's grave, there were similar large patches on Harold's and Luke's graves. Only William's and Randall's remained undisturbed now.

"Do you think the ghost is digging up the graves?" Colin asked.

"I—I don't know." I shivered. "Maybe it wasn't a ghost. I mean, they aren't supposed to be real."

"Then what was it?"

"I don't know. Fog? Reflection of the moon on the trees?"

"Yeah, right. You and I both know it had the shape of a person."

"Bigfoot," I offered.

"In a white robe?" He gripped his flashlight and shone it into the deep woods. "Let's go back."

I ran my flashlight back and forth on the ground. "Wait, look at that." My light reflected off something shimmering on a branch.

I went over to it. There was a small piece of gauzy white fabric about two inches long with glitter on it. The glitter came off in my hand and stuck to my fingers.

"I bet it's from the ghost," Colin said.

"Why would a ghost need glitter to make it sparkle?" I asked.

"Let's go back and talk about this at camp."

I nodded and followed him back to the trail.

We were on the edge of camp when a figure stepped into our path. Both Colin and I squealed and dropped our flashlights.

"Geez, relax," Ava said.

I scooped up our flashlights and handed Colin his. I shone my light in Ava's eyes.

"Hey!" she protested.

I lowered my flashlight. "Keep your voice down. Do you want to wake up the entire camp?"

"What are you two doing outside the tents in the middle of the night?" she asked.

"None of your business," I said.

"It's my business if it costs me an 'A' on this bird project. I decided to be in this group because I thought it was the best way to ace the assignment. I did you a favor by joining you."

"You act like we wanted you in the group," I said. As soon as the words were out of my mouth, I wanted to shove them back in.

"Oh, I know you didn't want me in the group. You made that very clear in Mr. McCone's classroom."

Colin jumped in between us. "Andi wanted to show me the graveyard that you saw earlier today."

Ava arched an eyebrow. "You believe in the ghost story?"

Colin opened his mouth, and I stepped squarely on his foot. There was no way I was letting him tell Ava about whatever we just saw in the woods.

Ava put her hand on her hip. "Did you see the ghost?"

He pulled his foot away but didn't answer. I think he got the hint.

When we didn't answer, Ava said, "Maybe the ghost of Dominika Shalley didn't feel like talking."

"Maybe," I agreed.

Ava moved the flashlight back and forth over us and examined both of our faces as if looking for any clue as to whether we were lying. "I'm going back to bed. Claudette's going to wake up in a few hours and I want more sleep. It's not easy with Andi snoring."

"I don't snore," I said.

She grinned. "How do you know?"

"My sister would have told me by now."

"Maybe she just doesn't want to hurt your feelings." She gave me a fake sweet smile.

"You don't know my sister," I said.

"Let's all go back to our tents," Colin said. "Tomorrow is going to be a long day, and we have a lot to think about." He gave me a meaningful look that I knew Ava didn't miss. She didn't miss most things.

Minutes later, I crawled back into my sleeping bag, but sleep didn't come. I kept wondering about what Colin and I had seen in the woods. It couldn't be a ghost. Ghosts didn't have to bedazzle their clothing to make it shine. If it wasn't a ghost, what or who was it?

I forced myself to think about something else or I would never be able to sleep. My thoughts turned to Ava, which wasn't any better. I know I hadn't tried to make her feel welcome in our group, and I was sorry for that. Throughout the dark night, I alternated between the guilt I deserved and the fear of something I didn't know if I believed.

Thump, thump, thump. Something smacked at the side of our tent. I sat bolt upright, but since I was burrowed so far into my sleeping bag, I fell over on top of Ava.

"Ahh!" she cried into her pillow. "Get off me!" She shoved me away, and I rolled to the other side of the tent and bounced off the nylon siding.

"What are you girls doing in there?" Claudette wanted to know. "It's five thirty. It's time to get up and hit the trails. I let you sleep in long enough."

"She let us sleep in?" Ava groaned. "What planet is she from?"

"I heard that," Claudette said from the other side of the tent.

I wriggled out of my sleeping bag and crawled to

the door of the tent. It was still dark. There was just the slightest hint of the sky lightening in the east. Sunrise wouldn't be for another hour and a half. Memories of what Colin and I saw came rushing back to me. It couldn't have been a real ghost. Ghosts didn't exist.

Colin stood beside his tent with his pack strapped to his back and his binoculars hanging from his neck. He appeared wide awake and ready to hit the trail like he had slept eight hours straight. I touched the top of my pink hair. It stood up in all directions.

"Move," Ava said from behind me.

I crawled away from the entrance of our tent and stood.

Claudette and Colin weren't the only ones up. All the birders were out of their tents and preparing for the search for the Kirtland's warbler.

Mr. McCone told us in science class on Friday that the Kirtland's warbler spent the winter in the Bahamas and the summer in Michigan. The bird crossed Ohio to travel back and forth between the two places, but since the bird was endangered, it was rarely spotted during migration. Seeing the Kirtland's this weekend would be a big deal for any birder, and if Colin, Ava, or I saw it, it would be twenty extra credit points. I started to get excited that we might actually succeed today. And at the same time, I tried to push the ghost sighting to the back of my mind.

Gregory stood a few feet away from his tent sipping coffee. He had an amused expression on his face while he watched the campers scramble to get ready.

"What are you smiling at?" Claudette asked.

"There's all this fuss about seeing the Kirtland's." His smile grew. "When I've already seen it."

"You're lying," Claudette accused.

He picked up a large camera with the longest lens I had ever seen from a camp table by his tent. "I have the proof right here."

A crowd of birders swarmed around him. Gregory turned on the camera and showed them the photo.

"Oh my," someone cried. "It *is* a Kirtland's. I wouldn't believe it if I didn't see it myself."

"I can't believe it," one of the triplets said. "Do you think it is still there? Where exactly did you see it?"

"And when?" another triplet, maybe Jim, asked.

I elbowed my way through the crowd. I wanted to see the proof too. I examined the shot. The bird was perched on a stone of some sort. It was zoomed in too much; I couldn't see what type of stone it was. The hairs on the back of my neck stood up. "Where was this taken?"

"Right here in the park." He turned off the camera and hung the strap around his head.

"When?" I asked. "It looks like it was at the grave-yard in the middle of the park."

He laughed. "Don't be ridiculous."

"The bird was sitting on a stone by the river. It flows about a half mile south of here. I saw it yesterday afternoon."

"Why didn't you say anything about it last night when we were all around the fire?" one of the triplets wanted to know.

Gregory turned off his camera. "And ruin your

retelling of Dominika Shalley's story? I didn't want to upstage you, Jim."

Jim frowned as if he wasn't sure he believed that. I wasn't sure I believed that either.

"So what if Gregory saw it first?" Claudette interrupted. "We'll have our own chance to see the Kirtland's. If Gregory can find it in these woods, then so can I."

Gregory smiled. "I find your overconfidence charming. Just be careful when you make an identification. We wouldn't want any embarrassing mistakes now, would we?"

Colin raised his eyebrows at me and I shrugged back. There was definitely some history between Gregory and Claudette. If Bergita wasn't going to tell me, I knew Claudette wouldn't say a word. I would have to find out another way.

A half hour later, the sun was still not fully up, but the early fall sky was a mix of purple, pink, and orange. I could have stood there and stared at it all day, but Claudette wasn't having that. She waited at the head of the path. "We're burning daylight, people!"

The three of us kids hiked our daypacks onto our backs and walked into the forest. With every step, I became more and more convinced that what Colin and I saw last night at the graveyard wasn't a ghost. Claudette had been right. The ghost story Jim told had gotten into our heads. Had one of the birders played a practical joke on us? If they had, they got us good.

Then again, I thought as I fell back in the line next to Bergita, I could always get a second opinion.

"Bergita," I whispered. "What do you think about Dominika Shalley and the ghost story? Do you think it could be true?"

She stepped over a rock in the middle of the path. "I don't believe it. Ghosts are just fancies of a person's imagination. It's a good story, and I do love a good story. I'm sure when someone sees the ghost, or thinks they see the ghost, it's really a trick of the light or a shadow. It's something perfectly mundane. However, when someone gets an idea in their head that a ghost is around, then that person sees the ghost because their mind is playing tricks on them."

I bit the inside of my lip. I couldn't tell Bergita that Colin and I had maybe seen the ghost. First of all, it would be admitting that we left our tents in the middle of the night, and second of all, she'd think we were crazy. The second was the worst. Bergita wouldn't be the least bit surprised that Colin and I went exploring.

Bergita sighed. "Claudette seems set on taking us on another death march today. I'll see if I can get her to slow down." She forged ahead.

Ava walked over to me. "You're asking a lot of questions about the ghost. Are you scared?"

I glared at her. "No."

"Could have fooled me," she said with a shrug. She joined Bergita and Claudette at the front of the line.

Technically, only Claudette, Ava, Colin, Bergita, and I were together in our quest to see the Kirtland's warbler, but as I looked behind me I saw a line of birders eight deep, including the triplets, following us. They paused when I turned around. Suddenly every last one of them brought their binoculars to their eyes like they were searching the trees for other birds.

We were being followed. I hurried to join the others at the beginning of the line. "Claudette, do you know you have other birders following you?"

"Don't worry about them," Claudette said, glaring at the group of shame-faced birders. "They think the best chance they have of seeing the Kirtland's is by following me. I always have a group of leeches on my tail feathers."

Ava rolled her eyes when Claudette said "tail feathers." I had to admit it was taking the whole birder thing a little far.

One of the people following us was Paige, Gregory's student. I wondered why she was with us instead of with Gregory.

Claudette, Bergita, Ava, and Colin went on, but I stood on the edge of the path and waited for Paige and the other followers to catch up.

"Beautiful day, isn't it?" one of the triplets said.

"It is. Is this good weather for birding?" I asked.

He smiled. "The very best. I have a good feeling about today. I think Claudette will finally see her Kirtland's."

"It is about time," another triplet said.

I kicked a twig off the path. "I know she's never seen one before and really wants to see this one."

The third triplet lowered his binoculars from scanning the treetops. "In a way, that's true."

By now, my group had disappeared around the bend. Most of the other birders including Paige had gone around the bend too. It was just me and the triplets. Today they wore matching navy blue windbreakers.

"What do you mean?" I asked.

"She claimed to have seen a Kirtland's warbler before. I believe it was at Magee Marsh, which is the best place for birding in Ohio, maybe in the entire country, during spring migration. We go every year, don't we, boys?"

The two other brothers agreed. "The very best birding."

"Where is it?" I asked.

"Western Ohio near Lake Erie. Thousands of songbirds stop there in May to recharge before they make the final long flight over the Great Lakes into Canada. It's especially known for warblers. We've seen countless warblers there." He sighed. "But never a Kirtland's, which is why we're here."

I could no longer hear the group ahead moving through the forest. They must have gotten a long way ahead of us now. I wanted to hear what the triplets had to say, but they were going to have to speed it up if we had any hope of catching up with the others. "But Claudette thought she saw one there?"

"Right." A triplet nodded. "I remember, it was at Magee, and there were almost a thousand birders, diehards and novices, there. Claudette called out that she saw a Kirtland's warbler, and of course, everyone rushed over to see." He shook his head. "But it was evident to at least one expert that it was a misidentification. You see, warblers are difficult to identify at times because there are so many hybrids. If a warbler can't find a mate of its exact species it will ..." He blushed. "Well, in any case, the expert said it was most definitely a hybrid. He suspected that the most prominent species in it was a Nashville warbler. The size of the bird was the first tip-off to the mistake. Even though Kirtland's are hard to spot, they are larger than most warblers. They are about six inches. Most warblers are four and three quarters. This bird was smaller than a Kirtland's."

"Were you there?"

They nodded in unison.

"We were," one of the brother's replied. "It was a thrilling, if eventually disappointing, event."

"When was this?" I asked.

He sucked on teeth. "I would say near about fifteen years ago."

My mouth fell open. "Fifteen years ago and people are still talking about it?"

"The birder community, the elite birding community, is small, and they remember. If they weren't at the misidentification themselves, they heard the story from another. But, of course, by now, all is forgiven. Claudette has seen so many birds in so many places in the world that the community respects her. She's a bit of a celebrity really." He lowered his voice. "Just between you, me, and my brothers here, I think she hasn't forgiven herself, so she is on this quest to see a Kirtland's."

"Oh, I think you are right," another triplet said.

"Very well said, Jack," the third agreed, and at least now I knew which one was Jack.

"You said everyone has forgiven Claudette now, but what happened right after the misidentification?" I asked.

Jack shook his head. "She was disgraced in the birder community. It took her years to rebuild her reputation as a top birder."

"She's been all over the world to prove it," another brother said.

"It must have cost her a fortune with all the travel costs," the third triplet agreed. "But she did it. She's dedicated her entire life to it."

His comment reminded me of the argument I had overheard between Claudette and Bergita about money.

"Who was the birder who proved her wrong?" I asked, even though I already knew. It could only be one person.

"Gregory," he said.

A bird song floated toward us.

"Oh!" Jack cried. "That's a palm warbler. We don't want to miss that. Come on, boys!" The triplets sprinted down the path with their daypacks bouncing on their backs the entire way. They could move pretty fast for three pudgy guys.

I didn't want to miss the palm warbler either so I followed them. I just made the turn in the bend of the road when Colin came running toward me. He was breathing hard. "Andi," Colin said breathless. "What are you doing? We thought you wandered off the trail. Bergita and I have been looking for you."

"Colin, take a breath," I ordered. "Do you need

to take a couple puffs of your inhaler? If you have an asthma attack because you were looking for me, Bergita will never forgive me."

He bent over, grabbed his knees, and breathed. "I'm okay." After a few deep breaths, he straightened up.

"Why were you so worried?" I asked. Colin was used to my disappearing when we were in the middle of investigations. I had to follow wherever the case may lead.

"I—I thought . . ." He blushed bright red. "You will think I'm stupid if I say it."

"No, I won't."

"I thought maybe whatever we saw last night—and I'm not saying that it was a ghost—got you."

I stared at him in disbelief. Colin was the most logical person I knew. If he believed in Dominika's ghost, then could it be true?

"I'm fine, Colin. I stopped to talk to one of the triplets, and I found out some information about Claudette and Gregory." Quickly, I told him what I learned as we went down the path.

Colin's face cleared. I knew it was because I didn't make fun of him over the ghost thing. Truth be told, I was starting to wonder about it myself. I felt in my jeans pocket for the little piece of glittery fabric. Ghosts don't need glitter, I reminded myself. At least, I hoped they didn't.

The palm warbler sang again.

I followed the bend and found all the birders plus Claudette, Bergita, and Ava staring at a bird in a young maple tree. Colin recorded the palm warbler in our assignment notebook.

"Colin, I think it's time we get out the casebook too." I patted the shoulder strap of my daypack. "It's in here."

He nodded seriously. "All these strange events call for a new investigation."

Hours later, we trudged back to camp, hot, tired, and without a sighting of the Kirtland's warbler.

Gregory leaned back in his lawn chair. "How did the expedition go, Claudette? I hope you at least saw a house sparrow."

Claudette stopped just short of growling at him. "We saw many varieties of birds. The children will have a long list to take back to their teacher."

A smile crossed his face. "But the Kirtland's warbler remains elusive. It's such a shame that you haven't seen one yet, Claudette. It's been too many years of searching. Maybe you should give up the quest."

Claudette glared down at him. "Shut your mouth, you pompous jerk!"

Gregory's smile didn't even waver. "Please don't

resort to name-calling in front of my students and in front of your young charges. We wouldn't want them to get the idea that such behavior is acceptable, now would we?"

"Help! Help!" Paige raced out of the woods and was holding her chest. "Help!"

Everyone turned and stared at her.

Gregory leapt out of his chair. "Paige! What's wrong? Are you hurt?"

"I ... I ..."

"Spit it out, girl!" Claudette ordered.

Gregory glared at Claudette. "Please don't address my student in that manner." He took Paige by the arm and lowered her into the chair he'd just left. "Are you all right?"

She nodded and looked up to find thirty people staring down at her. Her face turned bright red. "I had a terrible scare. I was in the woods. I planned to come back with everyone else, but I thought I heard an Eastern Towhee in the brush. I really wanted to get a good photo of one because they're my favorite bird. I was bent over searching the ground for it. You know they like to stay low."

"Yes, we all know that," Claudette snapped.

If possible, Paige's face turned even redder. "Right." She took a deep breath. "Anyway, I was rooting through the brush, and I must have wandered off the path, because the trail disappeared. Before long, I found myself in the graveyard."

A hush fell over the birders.

"You were in the Shalley cemetery?" Jack the

triplet asked. "You couldn't pay me to go there. The place is haunted."

His brothers nodded in agreement.

Paige licked her lips. "I didn't plan to be there. I stumbled into it. I wanted to get out. I was looking at the map to decide which direction led to camp, when a shadow fell over the paper." She shivered and her voice dropped low. We leaned in to hear what she was about to say next. "Then I saw her. She was on the far side of the graveyard, passing in the middle of the trees just beyond the ravine. I couldn't believe it. It was Dominika Shalley's ghost. I even pinched myself in case I was imagining it."

"I thought the ghost only came out at night," someone said.

Gregory started laughing. "Oh, Paige, that's a funny joke. You really had us going."

"I'm not joking," she said seriously. "I really did see the ghost of Dominika Shalley. She was just as you described, Jim. She wore a long white gauzy robe and had silver hair that cascaded down her back." She shivered again. "And she seemed to float through the trees. I've never seen a person move like that before, and I never want to see it again."

"How far away was the ghost?" Colin asked.

"It was pretty far, maybe thirty yards, and there were some trees in the way, but I did see her."

"How long was she there?" Spooner asked.

Paige grabbed Spooner's hand. "Maybe thirty seconds. It wasn't long, which makes me more convinced that it was a ghost. A person couldn't have moved out of my line of sight that fast. It would have had to be superhuman or a ghost."

"How can you be in college and think you saw a ghost?" Ava folded her arms.

Paige jumped out of her chair. "I know what I saw. And if you think I'm going back into those woods again, you're crazy." She stomped away.

Spooner and Susan went after her.

Gregory shook his head. "Young people are so excitable at times. Don't worry about Paige. She'll be fine. She's one of my best students, but she does have a wild imagination from time to time. Once, she claimed to see a cuckoo in the woods here." He laughed.

The other birders joined in. I wasn't sure what was so funny about seeing a cuckoo in Shalley Park, but the birders sure thought it was a riot.

I had to talk to Paige, either alone or with Colin. Her description of the ghost sounded a lot like what Colin and I had seen last night, but I wanted more details. Paige was the only person who could supply those.

A shiver ran down my spine. Another sighting of Dominika's ghost. Of course, no one else knew about what Colin and I had seen.

Gregory sighed. "I suppose I should go and check on my student." He went in the direction Paige and the other two college students had gone.

"Let's break for lunch," Bergita said. "It's been a long morning of birding."

I waited a few beats and then went in the direction of Paige and Gregory.

Paige was inside her tent, throwing things into her pack. Susan stood outside of the tent. "Paige, I think you're overreacting."

"Leave me alone, Susan."

She folded her arms. "It couldn't be a real ghost."

"I know what I saw." She threw a T-shirt into her bag.

"Then, it was someone playing a practical joke," Susan said.

Paige climbed out of the tent. "It was just so real. I know it's stupid to believe in ghosts, but I was so spooked."

"But—"

"Please, stop. If it wasn't a ghost, it was something else, something that didn't want me there. I can take a hint, so I'm leaving."

"I'm going to stay," Susan said.

"Fine." Paige slung her pack over her arm and marched toward the trail that led to the parking lot.

I followed Susan and Paige a few feet until I saw Gregory standing next to the Shalley's crumbling home. I walked up to him. "Paige left."

"That is unfortunate, but she'll be fine." The ornithologist held his binoculars to his eyes and searched the house. "Old stone structures are great places to see wrens and other small birds that like to hide in the brush. It's also a good place to see thrushes, which like to root through the thicket for worms and insects."

I folded my arms. "You don't believe Paige saw a ghost."

"I didn't say that. I'm a scientist, but I don't claim

to understand everything. I know enough to know that not everything in this world can be explained."

That was not the answer I expected to hear from a college professor.

"I do know Dominika Shalley's ghost would not have hurt Paige or any of us. She wouldn't have even shown herself unless she felt her sons' resting place was in jeopardy. As long as we stay away from her sons' graves, I think we can coexist with her. That's assuming she's real."

I squished my eyebrows together. I couldn't tell if Gregory was serious or if he was teasing me.

He lowered his binoculars. "I can see you are trying to sort this out. I always appreciate a scientific mind. If you have to look at this logically, follow the evidence. If Paige's claim doesn't make sense to you, then where doesn't it add up?"

I thought about this for a moment before saying, "You were the one who proved that Claudette misidentified a Kirtland's warbler in Magee Marsh. The triplets told me."

He grinned. "That was a long time ago. It's time we all forget and forgive Claudette for her mistake."

I narrowed my eyes. "Then why do you keep needling her about it?"

The grin fell from his face for a moment, but as soon as I blinked it was back in place. "You had better get back to Bergita and your friends. They'll wonder what happened to you."

I left the professor more confused about him and his relationship to Claudette than ever.

By late afternoon, most of the birders had either returned to the camping area where they would camp another night or gone home. Colin, Ava, and I struggled to force our tents back into their nylon cases while Bergita and Claudette argued a few feet from us. Although most of the campers were back, I noticed that Gregory and his three remaining students weren't wandering the campground. Their campsite was still up, so I knew they hadn't left the park. Could Gregory be seeing the Kirtland's at that very moment? We still hadn't seen it, but I was too tired to find out. After three long hikes with Claudette, I knew the seventy-some year-old woman could out-walk me any day.

Bergita rolled up her sleeping bag. "I wish you would come back to the house with us instead of spending another night in the woods, Claudette. I don't like the idea of you being here alone."

"I'll be fine. There are plenty of birders still staying here, and I've camped in much worse places by myself. I remember one particularly difficult night in the Galapagos."

Bergita tucked her silver braid under her ball cap. "I suppose I'm nervous after what happened to Paige."

Claudette opened a granola bar and took a bite. After she took a swig from her water bottle, she said, "The girl has an overactive imagination. I knew it wasn't a good idea for the triplets to tell that ridiculous tall tale about the Shalley ghost."

Bergita lifted her backpack off the ground. "All right, but if you get tired of sleeping on the ground, just come to the house at any hour."

"I'm sure your son and daughter-in-law would be thrilled to have me."

Bergita smiled. "They would be. And if you would like to come to church with us tomorrow, you are more than welcome."

Claudette took another bite of her granola bar and said nothing.

When Bergita, Ava, Colin, and I emerged from the woods, Ava's brother, Romero, was in the park's parking lot. Ava didn't exactly smile, but she did say, "I'll see you at school on Monday." She ran to the truck.

"Great!" Colin called after her. "Bye!"

I sighed. "I was hoping that we could bird some tomorrow after church. I guess Ava's not interested."

Bergita lifted our tents into the back of her station

wagon. "Andi, Ava has a lot more to worry about than school."

I added my pack to the back of the station wagon. "What does that mean? What else does she have to worry about?"

Bergita pursed her lips. "I think Ava will tell you when she is ready."

"What if she's never ready?" I asked and stepped out of the way as Colin added his pack to the pile of luggage in the car.

"I think she will be," Bergita said and walked to the driver's side door.

I stared at Colin. He shrugged and climbed into the backseat of the station wagon. I crawled in after him.

It was dark by the time we got home, and I was exhausted. Amelie flung open the front door as soon as Bergita turned her station wagon into the Carters' driveway.

"Finally, you're home. I was about to send out a search party," she said as soon as we were out of the car. Her delicate features broke into a smile. "Not that I didn't know Andi was in great hands with you, Bergita." She gave me a squeeze. "But I missed her."

My face squished into my aunt's armpit, and I had to wriggle free. Despite nearly being suffocated, I was happy that Amelie missed me even though I had only been gone one night.

Bergita laughed. "We had a great time. Andi was a treat as always, and I think there were some bridges built between her and Ava. The girls hardly argued."

Because we hardly spoke except for talking about the assignment or Ava accusing me of believing the ghost story.

"Where's your sister?" Amelie asked Bergita.

Bergita shook her head. "We didn't see the Kirtland's warbler, so she's spending another night in the woods. My sister is nothing if not determined." She stretched, then wrapped her arm around Colin's shoulders. "I'm beat. Come on, kid. Let's get cleaned up." She pointed at Amelie. "Church tomorrow. Don't forget. I'll come and pull you out of bed myself if necessary."

Amelie laughed, but we knew it wasn't an idle threat. Bergita had stormed our house before on Sunday morning, banging pots and pans to wake us up for church.

After waving good night to Bergita and Colin, I slung my pack over my shoulder and followed Amelie up the front steps into the house.

Amelie was in her yoga outfit and as soon as we stepped into the living room, she slid to the floor on her mat.

I dumped my pack on the floor by the front door. I wanted to go upstairs to my room and write down all I had learned that weekend in the casebook, but I was too tired to crawl up the stairs. I fell into my aunt's armchair, and a second later, Mr. Rochester was on my lap, kneading my stomach. I guess he missed me too. "Where's Bethany?"

Amelie grinned and tucked one leg behind her head like it was the most natural position in the world.

"She's at a party tonight at a friend from school's house. Isn't that great? I'm trying not to get my hopes up, but I think your sister is finally making friends in Killdeer. I so want her to be settled and happy."

"Who's the friend?"

Amelie's brow wrinkled. "Kelly, Katy, Kimmy, I don't know. I think it begins with a K. I was just so happy she said she was going to a party that the details are a little fuzzy."

"When is she coming home? What's her curfew?"

Amelie lowered her leg and folded her right knee over her left. "Do you think I should make one of those?"

"Probably." If Bethany had told my parents that she was heading to a party, she would have been interrogated about everyone who would be at the party and if there would be any adults in the house. It was just another example of how living with Amelie was different.

She folded her knees up to her chest and wrapped her arms around them. "So how was your trip?"

"Interesting."

She arched her brow. "How's that?"

I bit my lip, but then decided to tell my aunt about the ghost. "Do you know the story of Dominika Shalley?"

"Oh sure, every kid who grew up in Killdeer has heard that story." She bent into a full body stretch.

"Do you think it could be true? Do you think Dominika Shalley's ghost haunts the woods?"

My aunt looked up from her stretch. "Personally,

I have never seen the ghost, and your dad and I spent a lot of time in Shalley Park when we were children. It became a park when we were kids. Even then, your dad was interested in plants, so he would go into the woods looking for specimens. Most of the time, he would let me tag along and carry his bag. I loved every minute of it because I got to spend time with my big brother." She looked away for a moment but not before I saw the tears in her eyes.

Mr. Rochester hopped off me and bumped his head against Amelie's knee. He always knew when someone needed him.

I didn't want to start crying, so I asked, "Have you ever seen the graves?"

She stroked Mr. Rochester's orange fur. "Yes, many times. That was your father's favorite place to gather plants. There was less tree cover there, so more varieties of plants were able to grow. We never saw the ghost, but trust me, I looked." She paused. "I noticed that you took your dad's binoculars with you for the expedition."

"Maybe I shouldn't use them ... do you think?" I squeaked. "Something might happen to them."

"Don't be silly." She scratched Mr. Rochester under the chin. "I noticed because I knew how much your dad would love it that you were tramping through those woods just like he and I did as kids. It's a great way to honor his memory." Amelie smiled gently at me.

"Really?" I asked, glad the binoculars were in my backpack.

She grinned. "Absolutely, he would love it. Your

mom would too." She clapped her hands. "So, did you see it?"

I bit my lip, but finally told my aunt the whole story from Ava and me stumbling onto the graves to Colin and me possibly seeing the ghost in the middle of the night to Paige running out of the woods terrified. "Why would the ghost appear to us and not you?"

"Were you bothering the graves?" She placed Mr. Rochester in her lap, and the tabby curled up and shut his eyes. He would stay there all night if she didn't move.

I shook my head, remembering the holes I saw dug into the graves. "Colin and I didn't, but someone else might have." I told her about the holes.

"That could be it. What did the ghost look like?"

"She wore a white robe and had long silver hair. She seemed to float through the trees."

Amelie was thoughtful. "Did the clothes look old? I mean, if it was really Dominika Shalley from the Civil War era, shouldn't she be wearing Civil War era clothing?"

"It looked shimmery like it was made of silk or something like that. I didn't get that close to her to see if her robe was antique, but I found this." I reached into my pocket and brought out the piece of fabric I had found in the cemetery. Most of the glitter wore off, but there was still enough there.

Amelie took it from my hand. "Andi, this is polyester."

I gave her a blank stare.

"Polyester wasn't invented until the 1940s. I don't know who or what you saw in the woods, but if she was wearing this, it wasn't Dominika Shalley's ghost." She handed the piece of fabric back to me.

If it wasn't a ghost, who was playing a practical joke on Colin and me, and possibly Paige too?

Outside, a car pulled up in front of the house. I ran to the window to see who it was. Through the window I watched Romero open the passenger side door of his pickup for my sister. Bethany and Romero stood under the streetlight. She laughed at something he said and flipped her hair. A knot formed in my stomach.

"Andi, what are you staring at so hard?" Amelie padded to the window and stood next to me.

I pulled the curtain closed. "Bethany's home."

"Why isn't she coming inside?" She moved the curtain. When she saw who Bethany was talking to, she sighed. She rested her head against the cool windowpane. "I was hoping I could get through the first year of parenthood without having to deal with boys. And did he really have to be driving already? A pickup truck?" She shook her head. "I think that's a little harsh, don't you?"

I didn't think she wanted me to answer the question.

She stepped back from the window and the curtain fell back over the pane. "Maybe a curfew isn't a bad idea. Do you know who the boy is?"

"He's Ava's brother, Romero," I said. "He dropped Ava off at Colin's when we were planning out the birding trip on Thursday."

"Bethany told me she had a friend from school named Romero. I think she wanted to tell me about him before you got a chance. Maybe I was naïve to think they were just friends like you and Colin. She is fourteen." She sighed. "I'm happy she told me. I want to keep the lines of communication open. Your sister is too prone to shutting people out. That's the last thing I want to happen. I want you both to feel you can come and talk to me about anything." She put a hand on my shoulder. "You do know that, don't you?"

I forced a laugh. "I just told you I might have seen a ghost, so, yeah, I know it."

She laughed. "Why don't you go upstairs and hop in the shower? You need one after a night in the woods. I think you have a stick in your hair. It'll give me time to talk to your sister alone."

I planted my feet. "I want to know what's going on with Bethany and Ava's brother too."

"Please, Andi. Bethany isn't going to tell me anything about him with you hanging around."

I knew it was true, but it still hurt to hear my aunt say that. "Okay." I grabbed my backpack and ran upstairs and then up the second flight of stairs to my attic bedroom. I dropped my bag on my bedroom floor and ran back down to the second floor bathroom just as the front door slammed shut.

I turned on the shower in the bathroom, closed the bathroom door from the outside, and crept to the top of the stairs. I knew it was wrong to eavesdrop, but it was the only way I was going to find out what was going on with my sister. Like Amelie said, Bethany wasn't going to tell me anything. Mr. Rochester sat beside me at the top of the stairs. He was an excellent spy, and he knew all the secrets of the house.

"How was the party?" I heard Amelie ask.

"Okay," my sister answered.

"Did you meet some new friends?"

Bethany mumbled an answer.

"Who dropped you off in the truck?"

"Were you watching me?" Bethany's voice was louder and sharper than before.

"I heard a car and looked out the window, yes. Was that Romero?"

"Yes. He's a nice guy."

"I'm sure he is. Maybe next time he drops you off I can meet him?"

My sister said something that I couldn't hear.

"I was a teenage girl once too. I know what it's like, okay? Just let me know what's going on."

"Fine," Bethany said, but she didn't sound angry. "I'm going to my room."

I leapt back and dashed into the bathroom.

CASE FILE NO. 12

The next morning, I stepped into College Church and scanned the congregation for Mr. Finnigan. After some coaxing from Bergita, he had started going to our church a few weeks ago. I wanted to find my friend because if anyone could tell us the true story about Dominika Shalley's ghost, it would be the town curator.

"Where is he?" I swayed back and forth in the pew searching for Mr. Finnigan.

"Andi." Bergita touched my hand. "Stop bouncing around like a jackrabbit."

"I was hoping Mr. Finnigan would be here," I whispered.

"He might be. You can look for him after church. Now, face front and pay attention."

I sighed and looked forward. Bethany flipped her church bulletin over and over in her hands. I was dying to ask her about Romero, but I was too afraid it would turn into a fight.

Finally, church ended. After the pastor walked down the aisle, I jumped up and searched the congregation for Mr. Finnigan. He wasn't there. Disappointed, I followed Bergita, Colin, my aunt, and Bethany out of church.

On the drive home, I asked Bergita and Amelie if Colin and I could go to the museum to check on Mr. Finnigan.

Bethany rolled her eyes at my question. She thought it was weird that Colin and I spent so much time with the town curator. But then again, Bethany wasn't interested in history like we were.

Amelie frowned. "Patrick wasn't in church today for a reason."

"Shouldn't we find out what the reason is and make sure he's okay?" Colin asked.

"I see you have a bee in your bonnet about it." Bergita tapped the steering wheel then. "Yes, you kids can go over to the museum and check on Patrick. If he's not there or not up to visitors, I want you to come straight home." She pointed at Colin. "And you need to come home for Sunday supper. Your parents promised to be there."

Colin brightened at the thought of seeing his parents. They were both ER doctors at the local hospital, and he didn't see them often. Any time they ate dinner as a family was a special treat.

When we got home, Colin and I jumped on our bikes and rode to the museum. It was one place in Killdeer I knew well. I had spent a lot of time there since moving to town in June.

When we stepped inside the building, Mr. Finnigan unfolded his long legs from underneath the metal desk just inside the historical society's front door. He grinned when he saw us. "Andi, Colin, I have been wondering when the two of you would pop in again." He covered his face and sneezed, three times.

Colin and I took big steps back.

"Don't worry. I don't have a cold. It's these blasted allergies. The goldenrod is starting to bloom in the fields around town, and that is the worst for me." His eyes were red and his nose was runny. He dabbed at it with a handkerchief. "I skipped church today to spare everyone from my sneezes." He leaned on his desk as he shoved his handkerchief back into his pocket. "So tell me, what brings you here today?"

"Can you tell us everything you know about the Shalley family?" I asked.

Mr. Finnigan stood and walked down the smooth brick floor toward the archives. "That's a tall order. The Shalley family has almost as much written about them as the Pike family." He glanced at me. "And you personally know how far back the Pike family goes in this town."

"Are there still Shalleys living here?" I asked.

He shook his head. "There hasn't been since the Civil War. The five boys who were killed were the last of the line."

"Why is there so much written about them then?" Colin asked.

"Because of the ghost," I guessed.

Mr. Finnigan walked back to his desk near the entrance and sat. "I'm not one to give into fanciful stories. I like my history free and clear of folklore. But yes, Andi is right. There is a lot of interest in the Shalley story because of Dominika's ghost."

"One of the birders told us about her at the campfire on Friday night."

Mr. Finnigan rested his elbows on the desk. "Which one?"

"Jim. He's a triplet. His brothers are birders too and were there."

Mr. Finnigan nodded. "You must mean Jack, Jim, and Joe Higgins. I'm not surprised one of the triplets told the story. They love to be the center of attention."

"Do you know them?" I asked.

He nodded.

"Mr. Finnigan knows everyone," said Colin.

Mr. Finnigan shrugged. "Almost everyone."

"There was a professor at the campout too. Dr. Gregory Sparrow. Do you know him?" I asked.

Mr. Finnigan picked up his coffee mug from the table and took a sip before answering. "He's an ornithology professor at the university. I would expect him to be there if a rare bird was sighted in Shalley Park. I know him of course, but not as well as I know the faculty in the history department. That being said, one of his students came to see me last week. He wanted an early map of Shalley Park. Unfortunately, I didn't have anything like that. Until the land was donated to the city in the 1990s, there were no records of its trails and paths. They were only recorded when the land became public property."

"Do you believe the ghost story?" I asked.

Mr. Finnigan wrapped both hands around his coffee mug. "Of course, I love the idea of a sensational story like this in our little town. It could bring more tourists into Killdeer. But no, I don't believe that it's true. It goes against every logical thought I have."

"We saw the cemetery," I said. "There were fall mums planted there."

"That was me," Mr. Finnigan said. "It's one of my jobs to look after the graves, which is why I doubt there is a real ghost. I've never seen one, and I visit the graves once a month."

"We saw the ghost," Colin blurted out. "At least we thought we did until Andi found a clue."

Mr. Finnigan sat up straight. "What was that?"

Just like I did the night before, I removed the piece of fabric from my pocket. "This. We believe it is part of the ghost's dress."

He took it from my hand. "It's polyester with glitter."

"Amelie said it can't be from a ghost who dates back to the Civil War."

"She's right. Polyester was invented in 1941 in England. It didn't appear in clothing until 1950 if I remember correctly. I think you are dealing with an imposter."

"One of Gregory's students saw the ghost," I said.

"She was scared half to death. She actually left the camp."

Mr. Finnigan set the piece of fabric in front of him on the desk. "There are no such things as ghosts." He pointed at the piece of fabric. "And this proves it." He stood up. "If you want to learn more about the Shalley family, follow me." He headed into the old bottling factory.

I snatched the piece of fabric off his desk before following Mr. Finnigan and Colin into the hallway.

Near the end of the hall was Michael Pike III's office, which Mr. Finnigan had converted into the museum office and the place to keep the archives. He unlocked the door to Number Three's office. In its heyday, the building had been the Michael Pike Bottling Company, famous for their sweet ginger ale. The company went out of business nearly fifty years ago and eventually, the building was donated to the town. That's when it became the historical society and museum.

We stepped into what used to be the secretary's office. I could tell Mr. Finnigan had done a lot of work on it in the last few months. Instead of piles of boxes and crates all over the place, the display cases were polished and the artifacts, from Native American arrowheads to memorabilia from Michael Pike University, were carefully labeled. Even the bookshelves looked like they were in better shape. The books were upright and ready to be read. Mr. Finnigan walked to one of the shelves and ran his finger along the spines of the books, then suddenly stopped. "Here we go. Like I said,

I don't believe in the Dominika Shalley ghost story. However, ten years ago, a researcher came through and wrote a book about it. Here it is." He pulled a thin paperback book from the shelf.

The cover was a photograph of the crumbling Shalley homestead at dusk. Fog rolled in on the scene and there was a full moon. The book was creepier than the Shalley homestead was in real life.

Mr. Finnigan walked across the room and leaned on the desk. "Believe what you read in there with a kernel of doubt."

"Why?" Colin asked.

"The main focus of the book is the ghost story, but I would say the first fifty pages are a decent history of the Shalley family—how they came to Killdeer and why each boy decided to go off to war. You know, for the Civil War there was no draft in the North. No one was forced to fight. Many volunteered because they believed in the cause. There were other reasons, of course, that the men signed up, but that was the most common one." He sighed. "The last one hundred pages of the book talk about the ghost of Dominika Shalley."

Colin spun in a desk chair. "Can we talk to the man who wrote the book? Does he live nearby?"

Mr. Finnigan shook his head. "He passed away a couple of years ago. As far as I know, this is the last of his research. A year after his death, I contacted his widow and asked her if I could have his papers on the subject for the archives here, but she said she threw them all out." Mr. Finnigan winced as if the thought of all those lovely papers being thrown away caused him physical pain. "It's such a shame, so much town history was potentially lost."

Colin took the book from Mr. Finnigan's hand.

I leaned on the glass case. "You said that you visit the graves once a month."

Mr. Finnigan sat behind his desk. "That's right."

"Have you noticed digging in or around the graves?"

He sat up straight in his chair. "Digging? There shouldn't be any digging around the graves."

"We found holes," I said. "Shallow ones, but they are still there."

Mr. Finnigan jumped out of his seat. "That's an outrage and degradation of someone's final resting place!"

Colin and I stared at each other. We had never seen Mr. Finnigan mad before. Sad and guilty, yes, but never mad.

"We are trying to figure out who dug the holes," I said.

Finnigan rubbed his chin. "My number one suspect would be your polyester-wearing ghost."

I removed the piece of fabric from my pocket again and stared at it. "If we find out where this came from, it would crack the case wide open."

Colin held the book Mr. Finnigan gave him to his chest. "But how are we going to do that?"

"I haven't figured that out yet," I said as I tucked the fabric back into my pocket. "But don't worry, I will."

I unchained my bike from the lamppost outside of Mr. Finnigan's museum. "Colin, we have to go back to Shalley Park. I want to look at those holes in the graves again before it gets dark."

Colin straddled his bike. "But I told Bergita that I would go straight home after seeing Mr. Finnigan. My parents are coming home for dinner. You know how rare that is."

I swung my drawstring bag onto my back and climbed onto my bike. "It won't take long. I borrowed Amelie's camera, and I want to take photos of the holes."

Colin cocked his head. "You brought Amelie's camera. You were planning this expedition all along."

I grinned and kicked off the pavement. I was

halfway down the block when I heard Colin ride up behind me. I never doubted that he would come.

When we reached Shalley Park, we chained our bikes to the bike rack. There were still a few cars in the parking lot, but nothing like yesterday when all the birders within a hundred mile radius were there. At least, it felt that way. Of the birders who were still there, I expected to see Claudette among them, but her Jeep was missing. "Do you think Claudette went back to your house?" I asked Colin.

He shrugged, and we followed the now familiar trail to the cemetery.

When we reached the graveyard, I pointed at the ground. "Look, there are even more holes than before." I noticed at least three new holes between Harold and Randall's graves. I removed Amelie's camera from my bag and started snapping pictures.

Colin walked around the perimeter of the cemetery searching for any more signs of the ghost. "Ahh!" He screamed and disappeared behind a huge rhododendron bush at the edge of the ravine.

"Colin!" I cried.

His hand popped up over the bushes and waved back and forth. "I'm okay!"

I gasped. "I thought you fell over the side the ravine."

His head appeared over the bush. "Nope, but I think I found something." He waved me over.

I hung Amelie's camera from my neck and peered into the brush. I saw metal.

Colin reached down and pulled a metal detector from the weeds. "This is what tripped me up."

"Whoa," I said.

"Hold this." He thrust the metal detector at me. "There's more." He reached down again and came up with a short-handled spade.

"I think we found what's doing the digging," he said, holding the spade out to me.

I took it in my free hand. "We have the tools that are being used, but we don't know who is using them. Someone is robbing the graves."

I swallowed hard and looked at the tools I held.

Colin climbed out of the bushes and sneezed. "What are we going to do about it?"

"We can't let it go on," I said. "We have to put these somewhere that the grave robbers can't find them."

"We can take them home."

I shook my head. "We can't go riding through town holding a metal detector without attracting attention. Even if whoever is doing this doesn't see us, he is sure to hear about two kids on bikes wielding a metal detector and shovel."

"Maybe we should give them to the police then."

I twisted my mouth. "We don't know if a crime has been committed. Would the police even care?"

Colin nodded. "Or even worse, someone might think we were the ones digging up the graves." Colin tapped his foot down on the loose dirt over one of the freshly dug holes. "Whoever it is can't be digging for the bodies." He shivered. "I mean the holes are scattered all around the graves and most of them aren't bigger than my shoe."

I shook my head. "No, I think they are looking for pieces of metal around the graves, like maybe coins. That's why this metal detector."

"Like Civil War coins?"

"Maybe." I squatted next to a hole. "Or something else that's metal."

"Let's try it," Colin said and took the metal detector from my hand.

"Do you know how to work that thing?"

"Sure," he said. He pressed the button and the machine beeped to life. "Bergita bought one for us when we were in North Carolina last year, to look for coins on the beach." He ran the metal detector back and forth over the ground.

"Beep, beep, beep." The machine made the same noise as he waved it over each grave. When he reached William's grave, the beeping became more rapid until it made a long single wail.

"Here," Colin said. "There's something here."

I picked up the spade and knelt on the edge of William's grave. Before I touched the spade to the ground I stopped.

"What's wrong?"

I looked up at him. "It doesn't seem right to dig here."

"We're looking for evidence. If something valuable is here that's what the grave robbers are after."

"Right." I dipped the tip of the spade into the earth.

The first shovelful was just weeds and dirt and so was the second. Colin ran the metal detector over the exposed earth, and it went crazy. "You're getting close."

I dug two more shallow scoops before I saw the glint of metal.

With the tip of the spade I tried to tease the metal out of the earth. It was trapped under a shallow tree root, and wouldn't budge. The piece of metal was wedged too tightly under the root. I pulled at the root, loosening it just enough to pull the metal free. It was an old gold coin. I brushed the dirt away. I could just make out the outline of an eagle. I laid the coin on the grass and took a photograph. Flipping it over, I brushed away what dirt I could and took a photo of the other side. It was a person's profile, but there was too much dirt ground into the surface to make out the features.

"Hey," someone shouted. "What are you kids doing in there?"

"They're digging up the graves!" another voice cried.

I dropped the coin and jumped to my feet. Through the trees we saw a line of birders staring at us through their binoculars.

"Someone, call the police," the first voice said.

"Wait! Wait!" I waved my hands at them to stop. "We were digging to find out why someone else has been digging here."

"I don't think that helped," Colin said out the side of his mouth.

"She's lying," someone said. I couldn't see her face behind the massive binoculars.

"They are the reason Dominika Shalley's ghost

came back. They're disturbing the graves of the ghost's sons," the first man said.

All the birders began talking at once. I wished there was one face that I recognized in the group. There wasn't. This was not a good day for Claudette to take the afternoon off from birding.

"We aren't," I insisted. "We would never do that."

In the distance, I heard sirens.

"Bergita is going to kill me if we get arrested," Colin said.

"You and me both," I replied.

Colin and I sat in the back seat of the police officer's SUV with bars between us and Officer Handly.

I grabbed onto the bars. "Officer Handly, we didn't do it. We were investigating vandalism to the graves, not doing the vandalizing ourselves!"

He looked at me in the rearview mirror. He had laser-sharp green eyes. They were so green, I wondered if he wore contacts. I bet he got many kids to confess to things they didn't do with his steely emerald glare. "Likely story. You would be surprised how many kids your age I pick up in this town for vandalism misdemeanors. Kids have no respect for history."

"We do have a respect for history," I argued. "That's why we were there."

"Where are you taking us?" Colin asked.

Officer Handly dropped his gaze from the rearview mirror to the road. "I'm taking you back home and releasing you into the custody of your families."

Colin's eyes widened. "Maybe we should go to jail. It might not be so bad."

"We're not going to jail because," — I raised my voice — "we didn't do anything wrong."

"Tell that to your guardian," Officer Handly said.

I folded my arms and fell back onto my seat.

Too soon, the officer turned onto Dunlap Avenue. The moment Officer Handly turned the SUV into the Carters' driveway, Bergita ran out of the house. Across my yard, I saw Amelie running for us too. This wasn't good. Even worse, Colin's parents came out his front door. He took a quick intake of breath. I knew the last thing Colin would ever want was to disappoint the Drs. Carter.

Officer Handly climbed out of the car and spoke to the adults for a few minutes. I tried to open the back door but couldn't. The doors only opened from the outside. "I wish I could hear what they were saying."

"Whatever it is, my dad doesn't look happy." Colin twisted his hands together in his lap.

"You didn't do anything wrong. Bergita will holler at you, but then she'll get over it."

"I'm not worried about Bergita. Bergita gets over everything. It's my parents." Colin covered his face with his hands.

Through the windshield, I saw the front door of the Carters' house open again and Claudette stomped out. She stood on the front porch with her arms crossed.

"I'd be more worried about Claudette." I pointed her out to Colin. "She looks like she's ready to toss someone over the porch railing."

Colin peeked through his fingers and snickered.

After what seemed like months, Officer Handly let us out of his patrol car. As soon as I cleared the car door, I said, "We didn't do it."

Amelie walked over to me and wrapped an arm around my shoulder. "We know, Andi. We don't think you did anything wrong."

Colin's mother shook her head. "We are so disappointed in you, Colin. You never should have gone off to Shalley Park woods without telling an adult, and now, the police brought you home."

Beside me, Colin deflated like a popped balloon and stared at the tops of his shoes.

"What were you doing there?" Colin's mother asked.

Officer Handly removed the coin Colin and I dug up in the cemetery from his pocket. "They were digging this up."

"Only because we wanted to know what the grave robbers were after," I quickly put in.

He pocketed the gold coin again. "In any case, you should have reported the grave digging to the police and let *us* investigate what the thieves were after."

"Well, thank you for bringing them home, Officer." Colin's father shook the officer's hand.

"Dad—" Colin started to say.

"I wouldn't say anything right now if I were you," his father said.

The police officer nodded and returned to his SUV. He removed our bikes from the cruiser's bike rack before driving away, taking the Civil War coin I had found with him.

When the officer was gone, Claudette joined us. "What's going on?"

Colin's mother pointed at me. "This girl convinced my son to dig up the Shalley graveyard."

Claudette's mouth fell open, and she stared at us as though she didn't know us.

"Claudette, it's not true," I said. "We were trying to help. We found a metal detector and spade, plus lots of holes around the graves. Someone was digging in there. We used the metal detector to look for what the grave robbers were after."

"S-someone is digging up graves in Shalley Park?" Claudette asked.

"Yes," Colin said. "And we are trying to find out who it is."

"Y-you are?" She cleared her throat. "I don't think that's a good idea."

"For once," Colin's father said, "I agree with Aunt Claudette."

Claudette folded her arms. "I think we should all stay away from Shalley Park. If there is really someone there stealing from the cemetery, he must be dangerous."

Colin's mouth fell open. "But what about the Kirtland's?"

A pained expression crossed Claudette's face. "There will always be another chance to see a Kirtland's."

But Claudette had spent her entire life searching

for the Kirtland's warbler, hadn't she? How could she give it up now?

Bergita sighed. "It's been a long day. I think we need to all go home and regroup." She gave me a side hug and whispered in my ear, "Don't worry, Andi. I'll talk to Colin's parents. I always do."

I gave her a wobbly smile.

That night, back in my bedroom I snuggled into bed. It felt so nice not to be sleeping on the ground, but I wished that I was still in Shalley Park so that I could get to the bottom of this case.

I cracked open the book Mr. Finnigan had given us and began to read. Halfway through the first chapter, I fell asleep.

The next morning, I found the book flung open on the floor. I leaned over to pick it up. As I did, I found that it was in the middle of the last chapter.

I blinked sleep from my eyes and read. "When Dominika's last son died, the mother of five boys only lived another two years, still in deep mourning. In that two-year period, there was a rumor she buried coins and other trinkets in the ground near her sons' graves. Her husband was so worried about her doing this he planned to take her back to his hometown in New York for psychiatric treatment, but she died before the couple left Ohio, and two months after that, rumor began to circulate through the town. To this day, her ghost roams Shalley Park near what remains of the old Shalley homestead and the gravesites of her sons."

The coin! I hopped out of bed and removed Amelie's camera from my small backpack. Officer Handly had taken the coin, but I still had the pictures. I turned on the camera and studied the eagle side of the gold coin. It was the clearer of the two. I wished I could make out the features of the face on the other side of the coin.

Mr. Rochester bumped his orange head against my arm and meowed. Absently, I scratched him behind the ear.

If Dominika hid coins and other items from the Civil War in the ground near her sons' graves, they would be worth a lot of money now. At least, they might be. Mr. Finnigan would know, and if I knew Mr. Finnigan, he would know exactly what my eagle coin was worth too.

Mr. Rochester placed a white paw on my knee.

I looked into his green eyes. "Do you think I'm right, Mr. Rochester?"

He meowed loudly. I took that as a yes.

After I headed downstairs, I found my aunt and sister already in the kitchen. Amelie hovered over a mug of coffee with her eyes half-opened, but surprisingly Bethany was wide awake and smiling. That couldn't be good ... for me.

My sister broke off the corner of her piece of toast and held it between her fingers. "I heard you and super nerd next door got dropped off by the cops yesterday."

I went to the cupboard for the Lucky Charms. "Shut up, Bethany."

"Don't get me wrong, I think it's cute. You guys can have matching orange jumpsuits in prison."

Amelie took a swig from her coffee mug and grimaced. "I think this is yesterday's coffee. In any case, no one in this house is going to prison, ever, if I can help it." She turned to me. "Andi, I heard from Bergita last night. She was able to talk some sense into Colin's parents that you guys being brought home by Officer Handly wasn't completely your fault. Colin isn't to blame either. She promised his parents that she would drive Colin to school this week, so that you two have some time apart."

I opened my mouth to protest.

"I know it's crazy. Bergita knows it's crazy too. You will see Colin at school and have plenty of time to spend with him there and at home here when his parents are at the hospital, which is all the time. This will blow over. Just try to stay out of trouble for a little while."

"But—"

There was a honk outside.

Bethany hopped off her barstool. "When has Andi ever stayed out of trouble?"

The honk came again.

"That's my ride."

Amelie put down her coffee mug. "Ride? What ride? I thought I was dropping you and Andi off at school this morning."

"You can drop Andi off, but I have a ride with Romero."

My aunt blinked. "With Romero?"

Bethany swung her messenger bag over her shoulder. "Yes, I told you about it last night. You were just too worried about Andi being thrown in the slammer to pay any attention."

"I sort of remember that conversation," my aunt said. "But I didn't know that rides from Romero were going to start today."

The honk came again. It was three irritable beeps.

"I have to go." My sister walked out of the kitchen.

"Not so fast," Amelie said. "I'm not going to let you ride to school with Romero without meeting the boy first." She followed my sister out of the room, and I was close on her heels.

Bethany went through the front door. "Please don't embarrass me."

"Get used to it," Amelie said. "As your aunt, it's my job to embarrass you."

Bethany groaned.

Romero climbed out of his truck.

Amelie walked straight up to him holding out her hand. "Romero." She shook his hand. "I've heard so much about you. It's a pleasure to finally meet you. I'm Amelie, Bethany's aunt."

"He knows who you are," Bethany grumbled.

Romero dropped his hand. "Hi."

"I hear you will be taking my niece to school."

He nodded. "Yeah."

"That's very kind of you. How long have you been driving?" She cocked her head as if it were a casual question.

"I got my license last month."

Amelie winced. "You know to be careful, right? You use your blinker when you are turning a corner? You always wear a seatbelt?"

He swallowed and nodded.

"I know the school is only a few miles away, but cars can be dangerous machines. I don't want anything happening to Bethany."

His face twitched. "I wouldn't let Beth ever get hurt. I'm careful."

Amelie twirled one of her long curls around her finger as she thought.

I peered into the bed of the pickup. The only thing that was there was a duffel bag, a scratchy-looking blanket, and muddy footprints. There was a piece of a shimmery white cloth sticking out of the bag's zipper. I reached for it.

"Andi, what are you doing?" my sister asked.

Romero hurried over to the bed of the truck and threw the blanket over the duffel bag.

I jumped back. "Where's Ava?" I asked. "Don't you take her to school too?"

Romero's dark eyes left Bethany's face for just a moment and focused on me. "She had things to do. She won't be at school today."

"Why? Is she sick?"

Bethany glared at me. "Andi, stop being so nosy all the time."

"But, Ava is in my group, and I'm worried about her," I said, realizing for the first time this was true. Ava's sudden absences from school were a problem. Why didn't anyone else see that?

"Amelie," Bethany whined. "We're going to be late for school."

Amelie stepped back from the truck and wrapped her arm around my shoulders. "Okay, okay. You guys can go."

Bethany smiled, and Romero opened the passenger door for her.

After they left, Amelie said, "He opened the door for her. I'm taking that as a good sign that he is a gentleman."

I wasn't as sure. The shimmery fabric I saw peeking out of his duffel bag worried me. It looked familiar. I hoped I was wrong for my sister's sake.

She squeezed my shoulders. "We should get going or we'll both be late for class. And if I'm late, my students leave." She laughed.

Since Amelie usually took Bethany, Colin, and me to school, or Colin and I rode our bikes, it felt strange to walk into school by myself that morning. After stopping at my locker, I headed for my first class. Again, alone. Colin usually walked me to my first class, English, before going to Math. I didn't see Colin until lunchtime and was relieved when he smiled at me as I sat across from him at our usual table.

"I'm sorry I got you in trouble."

"Don't worry about it." He opened a bag of chips. "At least my parents are paying attention to me. That's a nice change."

I punctured the top of my juice box with its straw. "Amelie told me that we have to stay out of trouble or you'll be grounded." I sighed. "I guess that's the end of our investigation into Dominika Shalley's ghost."

"Why?" Colin yelped.

"Because you could get grounded."

"I don't care about that. It's more important that we get to the bottom of who is robbing those graves in Shalley Park."

"Really?"

"Of course."

I grinned. "Good. Because I discovered something this morning in Mr. Finnigan's book."

Colin leaned across the table. "Tell me."

I pulled out the book Mr. Finnigan had given us at the museum yesterday. A bookmark marked the right page. I opened it and slipped it across the table to Colin. "Read this page."

Colin ran his finger along the print as he read. He tapped the page with his index finger. "That coin you found and more like it are what the grave robber is after."

"Exactly, and I seriously doubt there is a real ghost. Whoever is stealing from the graves of Dominika Shalley's sons is trying to scare everyone away from the cemetery, so that he won't get caught."

"Who could it be?"

"I thought about that. On the night of the camp-out, who was excited about telling the ghost story that night?"

"The triplets?"

I nodded. "And Dr. Gregory Sparrow. He's the one who talked Jim the Triplet into telling the story."

Colin snapped his fingers. "You're right. It has to be Gregory. He's the one who keeps saying there is a ghost. He's the one who keeps warning us to stay away from the graveyard."

"Exactly."

"How are we going to prove it?" Colin asked.

I chewed my lip. "We need to talk to Paige. I bet Dr. Sparrow put her up to pretending she saw a ghost."

Colin licked Dorito dust from his ingers. "I don't know. She was pretty scared."

"We still need to ask her."

Colin nodded. "It's a lead. We can go right after school."

"What about your parents?"

He shrugged. "They won't be home until late."

I played with my juice box straw. "Okay. I'll email Amelie from computer lab in fifth period and tell her we want to come to campus after school to see her. She'll love it, and it'll give us a chance to find Paige."

"That's good cover. Great idea." Colin unwrapped his turkey sandwich and dug in his bag for Bergita's oatmeal cookies. He handed one to me.

"How will we find Paige on campus?"

"Leave that to me." I took a bite out of the cookie. After I swallowed I said, "There's another thing. Ava didn't come to school today."

"Is she sick?"

I shook my head. "Romero picked up my sister to drive her to school and said Ava was taking a day off."

"I wonder what's going on."

"Me too." I broke off another piece of cookie. "If

she keeps missing school, I don't know how we are going to finish the assignment. And we still haven't seen the Kirtland's warbler."

"It might be gone by now," Colin said. "Migrating birds don't stop over in one place for long."

"Let's hope you're wrong." I popped the rest of the cookie into my mouth.

During school that day, I couldn't wait to get to science. I wanted to hear the report on the number of birds the other groups had seen over the weekend, and I wanted to make plans with Colin about finding the Kirtland's warbler and the grave robber.

When I walked into the classroom, I was surprised to see Ava at her desk in the front row, but even more surprised to see Gregory Sparrow in the front of the room laughing with Mr. McCone.

I swung by Colin's seat on the way to my desk. "What's he doing here?" I hissed.

Colin shrugged.

The bell rang and I dashed to my seat. There was no more time to talk. Ava didn't even look at me as I passed her.

As soon as everyone was settled at their desks, Mr. McCone started grinning from ear to ear. "Class, I'm delighted, simply delighted, to have a guest speaker here with us today. Dr. Sparrow is an ornithology professor at the university. Apparently, some of you saw him at Shalley Park this weekend searching for the elusive Kirtland's warbler. Yesterday, I gave Dr. Sparrow a call to tell him about our birding project and asked if he would be willing to visit the class while we were working on this. I never expected him to come the next day." He beamed at the other man. "Thank you so much for being here."

Gregory shared a pleased smile. "It's my pleasure. I'm happy to be in a room full of young bird enthusiasts. It's nice to see Andi, Colin, and Ava again. We had a nice weekend together looking for the warbler, didn't we, kids?"

I shifted in my seat.

Mr. McCone smiled. "It's so exciting that a Kirtland's was spotted in the area." He glanced back at Gregory. "Did anyone spy it?"

"I did," the professor said. "Unfortunately, I was alone at the time, but I was able to take these great photographs." He tapped the SMART Board.

The bird was on a low branch of a bush and its beak was open in song. I wished so badly that I had been there to see it and to listen to it sing, but I knew Claudette, who spent the last fifteen years trying to redeem herself from her misidentification, wanted to see it more. That's why I had been so confused the night before. Claudette was willing to give up her chance to see the Kirtland's just because someone was stealing coins from the Shalley cemetery. She hadn't seemed like someone who scared easily. It didn't make sense.

Gregory clicked to the next photograph. "Some distinctive features of the Kirtland's warbler are its large size and blue-gray back."

"How did you find it when no one else did?" a girl asked.

Gregory turned to her. "I knew that the bird would most likely be close to the riverbank down low, and I got lucky. You see, when it comes to birding, luck is a huge factor, and I have always been extremely lucky in the number of birds I see. You can go out on a hike searching for a bird and never see one, or you can go out on a hike seeking one particular bird and see an entire flock of species. Patience and dedication to birding day after day is the key. When you do see the bird you're looking for, it is the best feeling in the world. It's the thrill of the discovery that keeps birders going. I had seen the Kirtland's on several occasions before, but I must say this sighting was the most special to me since it was right here in Carroll County. It was like the bird came to this county specifically for me."

Across the room, Colin and I shared a look and I rolled my eyes. He turned away and covered his mouth.

Gregory advanced the board to the next photograph. This one was of a Golden finch. "But there is more to birding than seeing one rare bird. Even the most common birds are amazing and truly wonderful.

We saw a number of species at Shalley Park this weekend."

"What about the ghost?" a boy at the back of the room asked. "Did you see the ghost?"

Gregory laughed. "I was wondering if someone would ask me about that. In fact, I hoped that someone would."

Mr. McCone laughed. "Now Dr. Sparrow, you know it's not very scientific to encourage children's flight of fancy when it comes to this ghost story."

Gregory grinned. "I know, and I would have agreed with you before this weekend. Now, I'm not so sure. There may be some truth to the story about Dominika Shalley's ghost."

Ava's hand shot up. "At the park, you acted like you didn't believe Paige. What changed your mind?"

"Who's Paige?" the boy in the back of the room asked.

Ava spun around in her seat to face the other student. "She's a college student who was there with Dr. Sparrow. She saw the ghost and came running into camp screaming about it. I've never seen someone so scared before."

The class took a collective gasp.

"I know, and I shouldn't have doubted Paige," the professor said. "I suppose as a scientist, I don't believe in something until I can see it with my own two eyes."

"You saw the ghost?" Colin blurted out.

"I did." Gregory lowered his voice. "I saw her. I was in the woods Sunday evening at dusk. Only a few birders remained at camp. Most had left for home hours before. I stayed behind because I wanted to go on one more solo bird walk before the weekend was over. I was in the trees near the Shalley family cemetery. Maybe I went that way out of curiosity. My student Paige had been so terrified by what she had seen there I thought I could find an explanation that would put her mind at ease. There had to be an explanation, or so I thought."

The classroom was so quiet I could hear the overhead lights hum.

Gregory waited for a moment longer. "Then, I saw her."

The kids in the class gasped.

"What did she look like?" a girl asked.

Gregory went on to describe the exact same figure that Colin and I had seen and that Paige had described when she came running into camp on Saturday.

Mr. McCone cleared his throat. "Dr. Sparrow, that is an interesting story, but it is just a story. We wouldn't want to put any fear into all these future scientists."

"I'm being perfectly honest. I saw the ghost."

When the bell rang that signified the end of the school day, kids from all over the classroom rushed up to Dr. Sparrow and shouted questions at him.

I gathered up my books and found Ava and Colin standing on either side of me. We were the only ones who didn't want to talk to the college professor.

"Ava," I said. "Romero said you weren't coming to school today."

"Well, I'm here. He told me that he drove your sister to school." She stepped closer to me. "Keep her away from him. She is a distraction we don't need right now."

My mouth fell open. "I can't control what my sister does any more than you can control your brother."

She scowled at me.

"We need to discuss when we can go out again and look for the Kirtland's warbler." Colin gripped the straps of his backpack.

Ava shook her head. "We don't need to go out again. I'm done. We've already seen more birds than everyone else in the class, and we will get an 'A'." She turned to go.

Ava wasn't trying to earn every last point of extra credit? It was like I didn't even know her.

I grabbed my backpack off the floor and followed her into the hallway. "Hey Ava, is something wrong?"

She turned around and I was surprised to see tears in her eyes.

"Tell us what is going on. Maybe we can help," I said.

"No one can help, especially not you." She wove through the students pouring from the classrooms and into the hallway until I couldn't see her any more.

Michael Pike University was only six blocks from the middle school and high school. Colin had called Bergita on his cell phone after lunch and told her we were going to the university to visit Amelie. She'd said it was all right but warned us to stay out of trouble.

As we walked under the brick archway that led onto campus, it still seemed weird to me to see so many students around. Bethany and I moved to Killdeer in the summer when there were only a few college students in town. Now there were over three thousand and the campus was buzzing with activity.

"Should we go see Amelie first?" Colin asked.

I shook my head. "Let's find Paige."

"You never told me how you plan to find her."

I smiled. "We'll ask Dr. Comfrey."

"Great idea!"

We headed to the science building. Dr. Comfrey was the chemistry professor who had taught us during Discovery Camp. Since Colin and I had helped her find out who was sabotaging her lab over the summer, she owed us a favor. I just hoped she hadn't gone home for the night.

We walked into the lab, and Dr. Comfrey sat at a lab table writing on a notepad. She looked up. "Andi, Colin, I haven't seen you guys in months. How are you?"

Colin grinned. "Great."

"Are you getting good grades?"

We both nodded.

"Excellent." She sat back on her stool. "What can I do for you?"

"We're looking for someone," I said.

"Ahh," the professor replied and hopped off her stool. She was a petite woman and her white lab coat nearly reached the floor. "Are you two solving another mystery?"

I ignored her question. "We met her last weekend. She was at Shalley Park with Dr. Sparrow. We thought you must know her because she's a science major. Her name is Paige."

"You must mean Paige Bingham," the chemistry professor said. "She's a biology major. I have her in biochem this semester. She's a double major actually. A very bright student. I have high hopes for her." A sad look passed over Dr. Comfrey's face. She had had trouble with brilliant chemistry students in the past.

"What's her other major?" Colin asked.

"Drama," Dr. Comfrey said. "I know that sounds like an odd combination. She told me once that her father wanted her to be a doctor and she wanted to be an actress. A double major was their compromise. I don't know what she'll do when it's time to graduate," she laughed.

I placed a hand on the counter. "She's an actress."

Dr. Comfrey nodded. "Yes, she had the lead in the school play last year. She's probably at the theater right now, rehearsing."

I was right. Gregory had put her up to pretending to see a ghost. It was the only explanation.

Colin and I thanked the chemistry professor and headed to the theater.

I had never been in the Creative and Dramatic Arts building, but luckily Colin had been there for the play last year and knew just where to go.

He pushed open the heavy door to the theater. Three students stood on the stage reading lines. One of them was Paige.

"Let's take five," an older woman at the foot of the stage called. "Troy, you have to enunciate better. I want to understand what you're saying."

Paige and her friends broke up. Paige sat on the edge of the stage and swung her feet while she read over her lines.

"Now's our chance," I whispered to Colin.

He nodded, and we walked down the center aisle to where Paige sat.

"Can we talk to you?" I asked.

She tucked a lock of her hair behind her ear. "Hey, you kids were at the park this weekend. What are you doing here?"

"We want to talk to you," Colin said.

"To me? Why?"

"Because we know you didn't really see a ghost on Saturday. You just pretended that you did."

She laughed. "Of course I didn't see a ghost. I was acting."

My mouth fell open. I hadn't expected her just to come right out and admit it. I glanced at Colin and he had the same expression that I did. "So you lied."

She arched one eyebrow. "It was a joke."

"A joke?" I asked.

She laughed. "Did you kids think I actually saw a ghost? Spooner dared me to do it just to be funny. I'm glad I was so convincing." She laughed harder.

"You didn't see a ghost," Colin said.

"No, there's no such thing as ghosts." Paige jumped off the edge of the stage and walked down the aisle toward the exit. Colin and I followed her. She placed her hand on the doorknob. "Now, you kids have to leave. I need to get back to rehearsal."

After she left, Colin dropped his hands to his sides. "That's not what I expected to hear."

"It still doesn't clear Gregory. I'm not taking him off my suspect list just yet."

"Good," Colin agreed. "Neither am I."

"Let's go find Amelie."

My aunt was in her tiny office buried behind a stack of papers and manila folders. "Andi and Colin, thank goodness you're here. This grading is going to be the death of me. I have forty-five papers to grade by Monday." She blew one of her curls out of her face. "And I thought grad school was hard." She jumped out of her seat and grabbed the top stack of papers. "Let's get going. I might as well grade at home where I'm more comfortable."

A half hour later, Amelie turned her car into the driveway. From the front passenger seat, I saw Colin's dad standing on the edge of the driveway with his arms folded across his chest. I winced. "Your dad is home."

"Yeah," Colin said glumly from the backseat.

Dr. Carter pursed his lips when we climbed out of the car. "Colin, get in the house."

"Dad, we were just—"

"I don't care what you were 'just'. Get in the house. Now." A muscle twitched in the doctor's jaw as he spoke.

Colin ran across the yard, and his father refolded his arms. "Amelie, I thought we agreed that Andi and Colin needed some time apart, so that they stay out of trouble."

"I was giving Colin a ride home."

"After he spent the afternoon with Andi," the angry doctor glared at me. "Please don't interfere with how I raise my son."

Amelie looked as if she wanted to say something in return, but she held her tongue as the doctor walked away.

● ● ●

The next morning, I woke up feeling dizzy. I had felt the same way in the days after my parents died. Of course, I still thought of my parents first when I woke up, I always did, but then I remembered how angry Colin's dad was the day before.

I reached the first floor just as I heard Romero honk the horn of his truck. Bethany flew out of the kitchen, through the living room, and out the front door. Amelie stood in the archway leading into the kitchen and shook her head. "I know I gave her permission to ride in his pickup, but I'm still terrified something will happen to her."

As soon as my aunt mentioned Romero's pickup, I remembered the duffel bag I saw in the bed of his truck. I ran to the window and watched them drive away. I had to see what was in that bag.

"You're nervous for her too, aren't you?" Amelie said.

Not exactly. I was worried about my sister. I was always worried about my sister. She was the last connection to the life I used to have with my parents. But I wasn't thinking about Bethany's safety at that moment. I was thinking about the duffel bag.

I saw Colin at lunch, but he muttered back one-word answers to my questions. His dad must have been really mad last night. Eventually, I gave up trying to talk to him and ate my lunch in silence.

The last period of the day, Life Science, was an oddly normal class. There was no special guest speaker, and Mr. McCone spent the entire time talking about bird bones.

When school was finally over, Colin came over to my desk. "Bergita is picking me up to take me home. I bet she would give you a ride too."

I shook my head. "Knowing our luck, your dad would be home again. I don't mind walking."

Colin and I walked to the front of the school. After spending twenty minutes convincing Bergita that I really did want to walk home, she finally accepted my answer. I waved to them as they drove away, but instead of heading to the sidewalk. I ran back inside and out of the back door of the building into the parking lot.

The middle school and high school shared the same parking lot, and I hoped that Romero's truck was still there. I had to find that duffel bag.

Most of the cars were gone. The high school released fifteen minutes before the middle school did. This used to drive Bethany crazy because she would have to wait for me so we could walk home together. She didn't have to wait anymore now that Romero was her transportation, but since it was Tuesday, I knew Bethany had Art Club. It was the only social group she'd joined at school.

Romero's truck was still in the lot. I bet she got him to go to art club too. I looked around the lot to make sure no one was watching. When I didn't see anyone, I sprinted for Romero's red pickup. On my tippy toes, I peered into the bed of the truck. The blanket was there, and I remembered the duffel bag I so desperately wanted to see was under it.

I stepped on the bumper and swung my leg over

the tailgate. I whipped the rough blanket aside. The bag was still there. I ripped open the zipper and pulled out the contents: a long silver wig and a white gauzy robe with glitter on it. I removed the piece of fabric I found in Shalley Park from my pocket. It matched. I pulled the robe all the way out and found a small tear in the sleeve. Although crumpled and worn from being inside my pocket, my piece fit into the tear perfectly.

I'd found the ghost.

I heard a shuffling sound, and peeked over the side of the truck. The school security guard moseyed in my direction, snapping a large wad of pink bubblegum. I didn't have time to climb out of the truck without being seen, so I threw the blanket over my head and hid.

I waited and listened. I was about to climb out of my hiding place, when I heard voices approaching the truck.

"Let me know how your mom is," I heard Bethany say. My sister was right outside of Romero's truck! Oh, this was bad. If she caught me, I was dead meat.

"I will," Romero said. "Thanks."

"And I'm sorry for my sister being so nosy," Bethany said.

"That's not your fault," Romero replied.

"She's a pain, but she's still my sister."

They were talking about *me* while standing right beside the truck bed where I was hiding.

Romero laughed. "Ava is nosy too. I think it's a little sister requirement."

Bethany sighed. "She's all I have left of my mom and dad too. I wish we got along better."

My heart started to beat faster, and I wondered if I should reveal myself. I didn't because I wanted to hear what else my sister had to say.

"I had better get back to Art Club," Bethany said.

Romero said good-bye, and a few moments later, the pickup door opened. And the engine started.

I peeked out from under the blanket. Above me, the tops of trees and the sky passed by. I knew we couldn't be too far from the school yet, but I couldn't tell where I was from just seeing the treetops and an occasional streetlight. If I knocked on the rear window of the pickup, I might scare Romero and cause an accident. I chewed on my lip. Aunt Amelie asked me to stay out of trouble. I don't think this is what she had in mind.

CASE FILE NO. 17

The pickup made a sharp turn, sending me slamming into the side of the truck. Gravel crunched under its tires as the truck slowed down. I crouched under the blanket and placed my hands on the floor, so I would be ready to spring up and out of there.

Finally, the truck rocked to a stop. I prayed that Romero didn't need anything from the back of his truck, but that prayer was short-lived because suddenly the blanket was ripped from my head.

"Ahhhh!" Romero screamed and jumped backward.

I scrambled to my feet, scooped up the duffel bag with the ghost costume, and hopped over the tailgate. I landed with a thud in the gravel. We were in the Shalley Park parking lot.

I turned to find Romero a few feet away. He had a

hand to his chest as if he were trying to hold his heart in place. "What were you doing in there?"

"What are you doing at Shalley Park?" I said back.

He dropped his hand and glared at the duffel bag in my hand. "Give that to me."

"No way," I yelled. "I have this as proof that you are the ghost and robbing those graves."

He lunged for the duffel bag, but I jumped out of his reach.

"You've been stealing from the graves!"

He held one hand with the other. "I need the money."

"For what? To take my sister out on a date?" I slung the strap of the duffel bag diagonally over my body.

"No," he snapped, stepping toward me. "Do you want to know why Ava misses so much school?"

I took two huge steps back. I was the closest to the path leading into the park. I didn't think I could outrun Romero, but I was willing to try. "Yes."

His jaw twitched. "It's because our mom is sick, really sick. Ava has been going with her to the doctor's appointments." He dropped his glare for just a second. "I—I can't. I can't handle going with her, so my little sister has to do it."

"What's wrong with her?" I whispered. My hand fell from the duffel bag's strap until I remembered I needed to keep it for evidence.

"Breast cancer. And all the pink ribbon support in the world isn't going to help her. She's going to die."

"B-but what about surgery or chemo? I thought they can fix this."

"Sure, they can try, but this is her second time around. Chances aren't that good."

Tears sprang to my eyes. I had lost my mother. It had been sudden and violent. She hadn't been sick. The day before she died, I had spoken to her on the phone. She had been healthy. She was in the best shape of her life. She could climb mountains and hike ravines, and I still lost her and my father. But I didn't watch her die. She was just gone. Was watching it worse? I didn't know.

"I'm sorry," I said.

"Yeah, well, now Ava is going to rip my head off because I told you. She doesn't want anyone to know, especially anyone from school." He scowled. "So don't go telling anyone."

"I won't," I promised.

"Good," he grunted. "Now, turn over the duffel bag."

"No way." I grabbed the strap again.

"You have to. I—I can't go to the doctor's with my mom like Ava can. I'm not that strong, but I can earn money to help pay for everything."

"By stealing?"

He glared at me, taking a few steps forward. "You're Beth's sister. I don't want to fight with you so just hand it over."

Before I could answer, a person came up behind Romero. "What is taking so long, Romero? This is the last night I can afford to spend on the site, and I want to get this over with," Claudette's familiar voice said harshly.

If the duffel bag hadn't been strapped across my body, I would have dropped it in shock.

"Claudette?" I whispered. "What are you doing here? You said we all needed to stay away from Shalley Park."

"Andi!" Her eyes snapped in my direction. "Yes, I told you to stay away from the park. It's for your own safety."

"Safety from you!" I shouted. "You used the story of Dominika's ghost to scare us away from the cemetery, so you could dig the graves up with Romero's help." It all made sense. Hadn't Mr. Finnigan said that greed was at the heart of this crime? Romero did it for money, money he can give his family. Claudette needed money too, but to finance her birding not to pay someone's hospital bills. I should have suspected her before, but I had been blinded by the fact she was Colin's aunt and Bergita's sister.

Colin's aunt waved her hands. "It's not what you think."

"It's exactly what I think," I said. "You stole coins from those graves for money to pay for your birding. You're still stealing from them." I looked from one to the other. "Isn't that what you are still doing?"

She glared at me. "Andi, you need to listen to reason. Give up the duffel bag, and Romero will take you home."

"No!" I cried and spun around. I ran at top speed for the trail leading into Shalley Park.

"Go after her," Claudette yelled. "You have to get that costume back or we'll both be ruined."

Behind me, I heard Romero crash into the forest. He would overtake me soon. His legs were much longer than mine.

"Andi," a voice called. "Over here!"

I paused for half a second to look around, and then out of nowhere, a hand yanked me into the bushes.

"Shh," Colin whispered in my ear.

Seconds later, Romero barreled down the path.

We waited for a couple of minutes crouched in the bushes. Finally, we crept out onto the path.

I knocked a leaf from my shoulder. "What are you doing here?"

"When you didn't come home after school, I had a feeling you came here. I arrived just as you were talking to Claudette and Romero." He shook his head and his hair fell over the top of his glasses. "I can't believe my aunt is in on this. We need to tell Bergita."

I shoved Romero's duffel bag back into the brush until it was so far in no one would see it from the path.

"What are you doing?"

"This is what they are after. I'm hiding it until we can find more evidence. This might not be enough to convince Officer Handly and the police."

Colin stared nervously up the path. "I think we need to leave the park, Andi."

"Not yet. We just need a little more proof that they're behind the grave robbing."

"So what should we do? Call the police?"

I shook my head. "No, call Bergita and ask her to come. If anyone can talk Claudette into doing the right thing it will be her sister."

"What am I supposed to say? Hey, Bergita, hurry up and get over here because your sister is a grave robber?"

I rolled my eyes. "Tell her that we are at Shalley Park, and we need her to meet us at the cemetery ASAP."

Colin sighed and called his grandmother. "Hi, Bergita. Yes, yes, I'm fine ... I know I should have told you I was leaving ... I'm at Shalley Park." He glanced at me. "Yes, Andi's here too. We need you to come here ... It has to do with the ghost and the grave robbery." He paused. "It'll be easier to explain when you get here."

I heard Bergita shout into the phone, and then Colin said good-bye. "She's on her way."

"Good. Now, we need to go to the cemetery and stop Romero and Claudette from taking anything else from the Shalley boys' graves."

From our many treks through Shalley Park the last few days, Colin and I knew exactly where the cemetery was. It was about a mile from the parking lot, deep in the woods. We walked there in silence, listening for any sound of Claudette or Romero on the trail.

We were about halfway there when I saw a figure to our left. I tapped Colin on the shoulder and put a finger to my lips. I pointed at the form moving through the trees. Sunlight reflected on the lens of the person's binoculars. "Ava! What are you doing here?" I called.

Ava dropped her binoculars and stared at us. She scooped her binoculars back up from the ground.

"Same thing you are, I'm looking for the Kirtland's warbler."

I frowned. "But you said you didn't want to look anymore, that the grade we already got was good enough."

"I know, but I got home and realized that I wasn't ready to give up, so I promised myself one more try."

"You could have told us," Colin said. "We would have come with you."

She scowled. "I wanted to do it alone."

"Colin and I aren't here for the Kirtland's warbler." I licked my lips. "We have bigger problems. We know who is stealing from the graves and who is pretending to be the ghost to scare us away."

"It's my aunt Claudette." Colin stared at the tops of his sneakers.

"And your brother, Romero," I added.

"My brother would never do that," Ava snapped.

Colin placed his hand on a low branch. "It's true. Andi found the ghost costume in his truck."

Ava folded her arms. "Impossible."

I chewed on my lip. "I know your mom is sick. Your brother told me."

Ava glared. "What do you know about it?"

"Romero said that you missed school to go with your mom to the doctor, and he helped Claudette because he needed the money for your family."

Angry tears filled Ava's eyes. "Don't pity me with that sad puppy look. You live in that great big house with your aunt and sister and don't have a care in the world. Meanwhile, I live in a tiny apartment with my brother, who doesn't care about anyone, and my mother, who is too sick to get out of bed most days."

"My life isn't perfect," I said.

She gave a bitter snort. "I know a perfect life when I see it."

"At least you have your mother," I snapped. "You can talk to her. What do you think I would give to do that?"

Ava jerked back as if I had slapped her.

"Come on, Colin." I marched back to the path.

Colin hurried after me.

"Where are you going?" Ava called after us.

"To stop Romero and Claudette," I said.

After a few paces, I glanced back and saw Ava trailing behind us.

We crept to the edge of the cemetery and hid behind a huge rhododendron bush about four feet from the edge of the ravine. I pointed to the drop, and both Colin and Ava nodded that they saw it.

Claudette and Romero were digging in Harold's grave. She ran a metal detector over the ground as he dug.

"That's Bergita's metal detector," Colin whispered. "Claudette must have gotten it out of our garage."

I nodded. That made sense since Officer Handly had confiscated the one Colin and I had been caught using on Sunday.

Claudette stepped away so that Romero could dig. "What were you doing with her sister? She never would have connected this to you if you hadn't been hanging around her family."

Romero plunged the spade into the earth. "I like Beth."

"I don't pay you to like anyone. I pay you to dig up artifacts that I can sell."

"Well, maybe I want to stop. It's just getting too weird and the police are involved. What if I tell the police what I know about you?" He folded his arms and smiled smugly. "That would be bad news for you."

She glared at him. "Then, they will ask why you didn't report me when you caught me digging in the woods in the first place."

Romero's face fell.

She smiled. "Wait till I tell them that you threatened to tell the police what I was up to unless I let you help me and gave you half of the money from selling the coins online. I don't think the police would look very kindly on that, do you?"

"Only to help my mom." He gripped his spade so tightly his knuckles turned white.

Claudette shrugged. "Do you think that will matter to the police? And who do you really think they would believe between the two of us? A juvenile delinquent or an upstanding elderly citizen?"

Romero looked down at the hole he was digging.

Claudette's lips curled into a smile. "I thought so."

Ava looked like she wanted to jump out of the trees and tackle Colin's aunt.

"I still can't believe Claudette is behind it," Colin whispered under his breath. "My own aunt stealing from those graves ... who knows how many other places she has stolen artifacts from over the years."

"I know," I whispered back.

"I found something." Romero reached his free hand into the hole and came up with a mud-covered coin. He held it up to Claudette.

She took it. Claudette rubbed dirt from the coin and held it up in the sunlight, breaking through the trees. It looked to be the same size and shape as the coin I had found. "Excellent. Another Liberty Gold Eagle coin. Pure gold from 1861." She grinned. "This one will fetch a good price online once I get it cleaned up. Good job, Romero. Now we can close up this site."

"What do we do?" Ava whispered.

"Bergita is on her way," I said. "She will talk some sense into Claudette."

"So my brother can take the fall." Ava glared at me. "I don't think so." She jumped out of the brush. "Romero!"

Her brother dropped his spade. "Ava?"

Colin and I joined her.

Romero looked at all three of us standing shoulder to shoulder. "You're with them?"

"What are you doing, Romero?" Ava put her hands on her hips.

Her brother scowled. "I'm helping our family."

"By stealing?" Colin asked.

"You're going to be in a lot of trouble," Ava said. "How can you put Mom through this now?"

"I was helping Mom."

"You were helping yourself," she countered.

Romero glared at Colin and me. "Where's the duffel bag?"

"I hid it," Colin said.

I groaned. I knew Colin wanted to take the heat off me, but he didn't need to do that.

"Where?"

"I'll never tell." Colin lifted his chin.

Romero dashed toward Colin, but Ava jumped in the way. In an instant, I watched her topple over the edge of the ravine.

I screamed, "Ava!"

Romero teetered on the edge and then stepped back. "Ava!"

Claudette put a hand to her face. "What did you do?"

"I—I didn't mean it." He peered over the edge.

I ran to edge of the ravine too. Ava was at the bottom moaning and holding her ankle. She wasn't that far down, maybe ten feet. But it looked as if her right ankle was bent at an odd angle.

"You had better go help her," Claudette said to Romero.

"Where are you going?" Romero asked.

"I'm leaving." She slipped the coin into her sweatshirt pocket.

"But what about my sister?" Romero cried.

"She'll be fine. I'm sure you kids will find a way to help her." She started for the path.

"Aunt Claudette." Colin's mouth fell open.

"I'm sorry, Colin, but this is how it must be. I can't afford to stay a moment longer." She jogged into the trees and disappeared.

I hesitated for a moment, wondering if I should go

after her. Instead, I grabbed Colin's arm. "Come on, we need to make sure Ava is okay."

I sat on the edge of the ravine. "The best way to get down will be to slide."

Colin put a hand on my arm. "Wait. I have a better way." He unshouldered his pack and removed Bergita's grappling hook.

I stared at it.

"I've had it in my pack all week, in case we needed it while birding. I forgot to take it out when we left camp." He secured the hook onto a young sturdy tree and handed me the coil of rope.

Holding the rope, I half walked-half skated down the slick, muddy bank.

Colin came down after me.

Romero didn't bother with the rope and ran down the ravine to reach his sister. It was a miracle he didn't break a leg in the process.

"Ava, are you okay?" Colin knelt beside her.

Tears streamed down Ava's face. "My ankle." She gritted her teeth.

"Is it broken?" I asked. I could already see her ankle swelling under her sock.

"I don't know," Ava snapped. "It hurts." She angrily brushed the tears from her cheeks.

Colin and I helped her sit up and then stand. Romero stood a few feet away frozen in place. "I can carry her up the hill," he finally said.

"Don't touch me." Ava wrapped her arms around Colin and me for support. "My friends will help me."

We made slow progress up the hill, gripping the

rope the entire time, and then down the path to the parking lot. Ava hopped on one foot and gritted her teeth. Romero walked behind us. A couple of times, I turned around and saw him wipe away a tear.

I knew Claudette would be long gone by now, out of the park, out of Killdeer, maybe even out of the state.

As we broke through the trees, I heard Bergita's voice. "How could you do this?"

"No one was using those artifacts. The dead don't need them. Why can't I make money selling them? Now get out of my way. I'm leaving," Claudette said.

"You're not going anywhere, sister." Bergita held up the spark plugs from what I assumed was Claudette's Jeep.

A siren wailed and two police cruisers, one driven by our pal Officer Handly, turned into the parking lot.

Claudette stared at her sister. "You called the police on your own sister."

"You didn't give me much of a choice."

The officers climbed out of their cruisers.

"What's going on here?" Officer Handly wanted to know. His eyes widened when he saw Colin and me, and I don't think it was because we were covered in mud. "You two again?"

"They didn't do anything wrong," Ava said through clenched teeth. She pointed at Claudette. "She's the one who has been robbing the graves, and my brother's been helping her."

"Don't be ridiculous," Claudette said. "As you can see the child is hurt and possibly delusional."

"I'm not hurt or delusional," Bergita said. "Ava's right. My sister's guilty of this crime, and it's not the first time, is it, sister? How else can you fund all those birding trips across the globe?" Her voice was filled with disappointment.

"Have you really done this other places?" Colin asked. "Have you stolen from historical places before?"

Claudette didn't answer.

"Ma'am," the burly officer said. "I would like to ask you a few questions."

"This is an outrage. I didn't do anything wrong!" Claudette yelled loud enough that I wondered if Bethany and Amelie heard her back home.

"She's lying," I said. "She has a coin in the pocket of her sweatshirt right now. She stole it from the cemetery."

Claudette glared at me.

"Please show me what's in your pocket, ma'am."

She didn't move.

Officer Handly walked up to her. "Hold out your arms."

Wordlessly, Claudette complied. Officer Handly fished in Claudette's sweatshirt pocket and came up with the muddy coin. "What's this?"

"I'm not saying another word without a lawyer." Claudette snapped her mouth closed.

Officer Handly shrugged as if it was no concern of his. "We are going to have to take you to the station." He removed handcuffs from the back of his duty belt. "You have the right—"

Nearby a bird broke into song, cutting the police

officer off. Claudette's head snapped up and stared at a nearby tree. The Kirtland's warbler sat on a branch a couple feet away singing his heart out. Claudette's hands flew to her heart, and her eyes fixed on the bird.

Officer Handly started telling Claudette her rights again, but it was clear she wasn't listening. She was staring at the bird. "It's so beautiful."

The Kirtland's warbler hopped to a lower branch, and tears sprang to Claudette's eyes. I bit my lip. What she did was wrong, but in a weird way, watching her stare at that bird, I knew why she did it. Birding really was her life.

As Officer Handly marched her to his squad car, she kept looking back over her shoulder at the bird. "I saw it. I saw it, and no one can take that away from me." Claudette said over and over again until the police officer closed the car door after her and we couldn't hear her any more.

EPILOGUE

I knocked on the apartment door and waited. Colin stood next to me and fidgeted from foot to foot. The door opened and a frail-looking woman with a blue scarf wrapped around her bald head opened the door. She smiled. "Hello, you must be Andi and Colin."

"Is Ava here?" I asked.

Ava's mother moved away from the doorway with unsteady shuffling steps. "She's in the living room. It's so nice of you to stop by. Please come in."

We followed her into the apartment. The brief entryway opened into a living room. Ava sat on the couch with her foot propped up on an ottoman.

"Hi," Colin and I said.

"Hi," Ava said back.

Colin held up the basket he was carrying. "It's from Bergita. She sent cookies."

Ava didn't take them, so Colin set them on the coffee table next to her foot.

Carefully and with the slightest wince, Mrs. Gomez lowered herself onto the couch next to her daughter. She chuckled. "More sweets. Everyone has been so kind to us since my relapse. I have eaten more sugar in the last month than I have my whole life." She smiled. "And I intend to enjoy every last bite."

"We came by to thank you. Thanks for jumping in front of me at the cemetery," Colin said to Ava.

"Yes, thanks," I added. "It was really brave to stand up to your own brother like that."

"It's no big deal," Ava said, but her cheeks were pink.

Her mom reached over and tucked her daughter's long dark hair behind her ear. "Ava is my modest girl."

Modest?

"She is always there for me. I'm glad she was there for her friends." Tears were in Mrs. Gomez's eyes. "And I'm so sorry about what Romero put you through. He feels terrible about what happened. He was only trying to help our family. Sometimes he just doesn't know the right way to do it."

"Will he get in trouble?" Colin asked.

Mrs. Gomez gave us a sad smile. "Claudette took most of the blame, but Romero has community service to do. He and Bethany were going over the list of places he could serve it earlier this morning." She looked at me. "Your sister is a good influence on him."

"Thanks," I said. It was odd to think Bethany was a good influence on anyone, but ever since I had heard her tell Romero she wished she and I got along better, I had tried to cut her more slack.

Mrs. Gomez turned to Colin. "I'm sorry about your aunt, Colin."

Colin flinched. "It's weird to think my aunt is in prison for stealing, and that she's going to be there at least two years. Her lawyer thinks she will get out early, unless she does something else wrong."

Ava's mother slowly rose to her feet. "Anyway, enough of that unpleasant talk. There is too much sadness in this world as it is. How do you kids feel about cheesecake? A lady from church just dropped off a chocolate strawberry one. There is no way Ava and I will be able to eat it all."

"Cheesecake?" Colin asked. "I love cheesecake. I can help you."

Mrs. Gomez laughed. "All right. You can lick the knife after I cut it too."

"Awesome." Colin followed her out of the room.

I perched on an armchair. "How's your ankle?"

"It's okay. The doctor said it's only a bad sprain."

"Too bad. That won't get you out of gym class for very long."

She laughed. "That's exactly what I thought."

I smiled, and after a beat, I asked, "Friends?"

"Friends." Ava leaned back in her seat. "But don't think I won't beat you when science fair season rolls around."

We would see about that.

ACKNOWLEDGMENTS

To my readers, young and old, this book would have never have happened without your support of my work and your love of mysteries. Thank you!

Undying thanks to my agent, Nicole Resciniti, who always goes above the call as an agent and friend. And thanks to my first reader, Molly Carroll, for your enthusiasm for all my books, and to my dear friend Mariellyn Grace, who helps me plot when I'm stuck, which happens often.

Gratitude to my editors, Mary Hassinger and Jillian Manning, and everyone at Zonderkidz. It's been a pleasure to work with you.

A special thank you to my brother, Andrew Flower, and my friend, Sarah Preston, both of whom are avid birders. Thanks for answering my endless bird questions and giving me the idea for this mystery. May you both see the Kirtland's warbler someday.

Love to my family, Andy, Nicole, Isabella, and

Andrew for taking me tent camping in the woods for the experience. Some of what I learned ended up in the book. You may turn me into a camper yet. Then again, probably not.

Finally, I thank God for Creation. May there always be a world with beautiful birds to admire.

Andi Boggs Series

By Amanda Flower

"In the upstanding tradition of Nancy Drew and Harriet the Spy, Andi is spunky and unafraid to take risks."

—Booklist

Andi Unexpected

Hardcover | $10.99

Andi Under Pressure

Hardcover | $10.99

Andi Unstoppable

Hardcover | $10.99

Available in stores and online!